The Master's House

Chuck Williams

The Master's House

Published by The Nazca Plains Corporation
Las Vegas, Nevada
2006

ISBN: 1-887895-19-1

Published by

The Nazca Plains Corporation ®
4640 Paradise Rd, Suite 141
Las Vegas NV 89109-8000

PUBLISHER'S NOTE
The Master's House is a work of fiction created wholly by the author's imagination. All characters are fictional and any resemblance to any persons living or deceased is purely by accident. No portion of this book reflects any real person or events.

Cover Art by Ross Johnston
Editor, Blake Stephens

Dedication

To David, the once and future slave, who has been tested in the fire of life.

Acknowledgments

This book was almost never written, and wouldn't have been without the help and support of so many people. A special thanks to Ross Johnston for the wonderful artwork on the covers of these novels. Secondly, thanks to all of the people that I have met in the leather community who have provided me with raw material to work with in creating these characters. In the local community, a special thanks to Jim Cassara who, of late, has joined me in my adventures. The people even closer to home who have had to put up with my artistic temperament, Jim Greco and his lover, Dean. And last, but certainly not least, to Michael English, my lover and sometimes slave, who guides my thoughts and gives meaning to my words.

The Master's House

Chuck Williams

Contents

Chapter 1

"Well, I think that the least an ex-lover should do is to have the decency to either die or move, preferably to Europe," the young man said to his companion across the table as he smoked his cigarette, much in the fashion of Bette Davis.

At the next table over, Lee and Colin sat, trying hard not to openly laugh out loud at the conversation that the two younger men were having. Even though it was November, it was pleasant enough in New Orleans for them to be sitting outside at the *Café du Monde*. Colin welcomed the sun and the warmth, a drastic change from the cold grayness of Columbus.

"Isn't it interesting that you and I are down here attending a funeral and those boys want their ex-lovers to die?" Lee said in a conspiratorial tone to Colin.

"I think that they might be a little too young for that to have the same meaning for them that it does for you and me," Colin answered, staring out into the crowds undulating through the narrow streets of the French Quarter.

"I wasn't complaining, Colin. Actually, I'm not so sure that it isn't a bad idea."

"Lee! You, of all people, should know better."

The conversation stopped abruptly. The two of them had been in New Orleans for three days, and many times during their stay, conversations would begin, and then end as abruptly as this one had. Colin didn't seem to be aware of the quick endings to conversations with his old friend, but Lee certainly felt it; almost like a kick in the stomach from such a dear and old friend as Colin.

"Colin, can I ask you a question?" Lee asked, staring at his friend.

"Of course you can, you don't have to be so formal with me."

"Well, that's just it. Usually you and I are so thrilled to get the chance to talk to one another that we never run out of things to say. These past few days, it's been difficult to engage you in anything more than a conversation that barely breaks the surface. Is there something wrong?"

"You mean anything more wrong than the fact that we've lost another friend to this horrible disease? Really Lee, we are here for a funeral. And we have been almost constant companions since we left he airport a few days ago. We've talked."

"Well, you mean constant except for the time that you spent with that little Latin boy last night?"

"A mere trifle Lee, but he was certainly more than a boy."

"See. Now this is better. Give me the details."

"Oh for heaven's sake Lee, he was hot. We had sex. It was great."

"Do you feel guilty at all? I can't imagine how. How many lovers do you have back in Columbus now, all under the same roof?"

"I have two lovers back in Columbus, Lee; and two friends who live on the third floor. And my cousin who lives next door."

"And haven't you slept with all of them?"

"You and I have slept together. Does that mean, because we are together, that you and I are lovers as well?"

"Well Colin, you should know that I'm game."

"Please. I have enough right now Lee. You know that."

"Something wrong in Camelot, my Lord?"

"It's Derek. He's really being bitchy, and somewhat ambivalent about me. He's even, on occasion, been outright hostile towards me. Our sex life is under whelming at the moment, and I simply don't know what to think."

"Seven year doldrums?"

"I'm not sure what's happening."

"Another man?"

"Let's not talk about it at all right now. Let's just go out and party tonight. After all, we are in New Orleans."

"OK, but I have some news."

"What is that?"

"Michael has taken a position at OSU next quarter. We're moving to Columbus."

"Lee, that's great! Try to get into our neighborhood. It will be great to have you two back as neighbors again."

"We did better than that, Colin. We're moving two doors down from you. Michael arranged the whole thing from Philadelphia."

"I am *so* happy. I can't wait to tell Derek and Al. Oh, I forgot, you don't know Al. But you do know Billy. He will be glad as well."

"Please keep Billy away from Michael."

"He has a lover, Lee."

Later that night, Colin and Lee went out on the town. They had a great dinner and then went dancing at the local gay dance bar. They followed this by the traditional bar crawl, replete with beads, ending up, drunk, in the baths of New Orleans. Both of them did things that night that they would regret the next morning. Luckily neither of them did anything that would seriously or permanently compromise their health. After all, they were two gay men in their forties; they knew better. The next morning found them with large brimmed hats and dark glasses, munching on beignets, again at the *Café du Monde.* When they felt that they were sufficiently recovered, they returned to their hotel, packed their belongings, and left for the airport. Lee's flight was first and they said goodbye in the terminal. Colin was left alone to feel sorry for himself. Sorry that he was hung over and sorry that his relationship was in some sort of state. He wasn't exactly sure what kind of state; the only word that he could use to describe it was, bleak.

His flight back to Columbus was made somewhat more palatable due to the fact that the plane was not crowded, and his seatmate was a gorgeous Italian man in his twenties. They spent the entire flight chatting; Colin was melting as he stared into the younger man's dark eyes and listened to his lilting Italian accent. The two formed an instant friendship; the encounter ended up with Colin offering to help the younger man find his way in Columbus. He was going to attend OSU as a graduate student. They exchanged numbers, Colin using his cell phone number, instead of the number at the house. He did it really without thinking, and only later wondered what had impelled him to use *that* number. They parted as they got off the plane. At the baggage claim, Al was waiting for Colin.

"Did you have a good flight?" he asked his Master.

"Yes boy, I did."

Neither man said much to the other as they drove home. Al realized that Colin had just come back from a funeral, he also knew that Derek had been somewhat difficult lately, and he had been able to feel the tension between the two of them the past few months. Finally, when they drove into the driveway, Al said, "It's good to have you home, Sir."

Colin got out and made no attempt to retrieve the luggage. That was clearly Al's job. Colin walked through the house, empty except for the dog that followed him from room to room. Al also knew that Colin was searching for Derek, hoping that his lover would greet him. He was nowhere to be found. Al knew enough to keep quiet and wait for Colin to address him. When Colin was upset about anything, strict leather protocol often prevailed.

Colin, for his part, was too proud to ask Al where Derek might be. It wasn't until much later, well past midnight that Derek arrived at home to find Colin at his desk, reading. He entered the room and kissed Colin lightly on the head. "Hey, welcome back."

"Where have you been, Derek?"

"I had quite a bit of work to do, Colin. Nice way to greet me after a week's absence."

"You're greeting was much better than the one I received when I got home."

"I told you I was busy!"

"Look, boy....."

Before he could finish, Derek cut in, "Colin, don't start the leather thing with me right now. I'm just not in the mood for it, and I doubt that you could sufficiently carry it out."

Colin turned to stone. He stared into the space right above Derek's head for a minute, and then turned his gaze toward Derek. The blueness of his eyes almost glowed. Derek couldn't hold his gaze for long, and turned his head away, saying only, "I have to get some sleep."

Colin eventually joined his two lovers in their bed. Both were asleep when he got in, and only Al turned to welcome him unconsciously into their fold. Derek slept like a log. Colin didn't sleep very well that night. When he got up the next morning, Derek was already gone and Al was preparing him some breakfast.

Over breakfast, Colin and Al discussed the trip, the funeral, and the household. Noticeably absent from the conversations were discussions about Derek. Al didn't feel comfortable broaching the subject with his lover/Master and Colin just didn't want to get into it with Al. After breakfast, Al left for school and Colin called to check in with his consulting company. As he expected, it was running beautifully. His concept had worked. Somehow, he had managed to bring together enough medical experts to form a company that more or less worked, even if he didn't dedicate himself 100% all of the time. And, it was lucrative.

As he sat at the kitchen table going through his mail, Billy bounded down the back stairs and gave him a big kiss.

"It's so good to have you home again," the young boy said.

"It's good to be back, Billy. How's Dan?"

"He's doing fine. He left for work rather early this morning, so you'll have to wait until this evening to see him. And I'm late for the bookstore, so have a good day and I'll see you tonight." Billy grabbed a jacket and off he went.

Colin had just decided to settle into his deserted home when he heard the knock on the back door. He went to answer it and was greeted by Dominic, his cousin and next door neighbor. The two men embraced and sat down at the table.

"What's up between you and Derek?" Dominic asked.

"Well, so much for small talk from you. What is it with everyone around here? No questions about my dead friend, my trip to New Orleans, just what's wrong with Derek."

"Do we need to have small talk Colin?"

"No, we don't. The truth is, I don't know what's up with Derek. He's really distant, and almost hostile most of the time."

"Is there someone else?" Dominic asked.

"I doubt that he would do it. Maybe it's a spiritual crisis. I'm not sure. He won't talk. When I ask what's wrong I always get the same answer, 'I'm too busy. I'm tired.' I've given up asking any more."

"Well Colin, I think that it's serious. Billy and Dan are talking about it. I've noticed it. Most people have. You have to do something."

"I don't want to loose him. I changed my whole life for

him."

"And he has changed his for you."

Dominic stood to leave. He grabbed Colin around the neck and tousled his hair. "Well cousin, you have to do something soon." He let himself out the back door, leaving Colin sitting alone at the kitchen table.

Colin was still sitting there when he heard the front door opening. Derek walked into the room, and, not expecting Colin to be home, was startled to find him there. "What are you doing here?"

"It's still my home Derek."

"That's not what I meant, you know that. I just meant, why are you home and not at the office today?"

"The office is doing OK without me. I needed a little time. Sit down." Colin proceeded to try to ask Derek what was wrong, but he got the same answers that he had been given for the past several weeks. He noticed that Derek wouldn't look him in the eye when they talked, that he would yawn frequently and turn his head from side to side. Obviously Derek wasn't going to give up any personal information to Colin at this point.

At one point, Colin initiated sex with his lover. It was over almost before it began, and while there was proof positive that both men reached the goal of climax, both of them seemed to be less fulfilled after it was over than before it began. No sooner had they finished when Derek blurted out, "I've got to get back to the church. I have a ton of work to finish." And, jumping out of bed, he dressed and hurried out the door.

Colin spent the day preparing dinner. It was elaborate. He called Billy, Dan, and Dominic and invited them over to join him, Derek and Al. When the six of them finally came together for dinner, it was like old times. Everyone was jovial, of course, the vast quantities of wine that was flowing helped the situation along.

"What was New Orleans like?" Billy asked.

"Decadent!" was Colin's only answer.

"I want to go. Can we go Daniel?" Billy asked his lover.

"In time, boy, in time," Daniel answered as he gave Colin the look of death.

"Well, I'm sure that you had a wonderfully decadent time

down there," Derek interjected.

"Not as decadent as you would think," Colin replied, reaching for his lover's hand.

"I don't want the details. What we don't know can't hurt us," he said as he pulled his hand away.

"I have some interesting news," Colin continued. "Lee and Michael are moving to Columbus. Michael has taken a faculty position at OSU and they are moving somewhere on our street."

"I wonder if they bought the house right next to mine," Dominic asked.

"I bet they did. He said it was only a couple of houses away from our address."

"Really Colin. Must you set about building this ideal community of gay men, all of whom are dedicated to you? It's becoming like a religion or a cult," Derek said without a hint of humor in his voice.

"I had nothing to do with it. I was just informed."

"I'm sure that if Lee was involved, he made sure that he and Michael would be somewhere very close to you. The man is in love with you, Colin," Derek continued.

"Come on guys. Let's talk about New Orleans," Billy said, trying to defuse the situation.

Colin was so thankful for Billy's interference. The tension between him and Derek was becoming unbearable. They would have to have a conversation soon that didn't end up with Derek avoiding the issues. As the other men cleared the table, Colin sat there wondering what was wrong. He couldn't blame it entirely on Derek. He had made mistakes himself during the relationship. Derek wasn't even behaving in his usually effusive self to Al. That was what was perplexing in the whole thing. Al had more or less been Derek's idea, and now he sat there in the relationship, much like a piece of art that had been purchased on impulse and now was waiting for a place to be hung.

As Colin was walking Finocchio that night, his cell phone rang. It was still in his jacket pocket.

"Hello, Colin. This is Chris," said the musically accented Italian boy.

"Chris. It's so nice to hear from you. Are you settling into

Columbus?"

"Yes I am. But it's terribly cold here, and there never seems to be any sunshine."

"Well Chris, Columbus is like that a lot. Gray!"

"How depressing. But I was wondering. Would you like to come over and see my apartment?"

"When?"

"Right now."

Under normal circumstances, Colin wouldn't have ever considered going out somewhere alone this late in the evening. He just didn't do that to his lovers. But the situation seemed to have changed at home. "OK, give me about an hour."

"OK."

Chris gave him the address and Colin returned home. He fed the dog and checked upstairs with his lovers. Al was studying intensely and Derek was already asleep; so much for feeling like a part of a loving and caring family. He put his jacket back on and went outside and got into the car. Colin had never behaved this way before. He never just left without saying anything. He would never go running after a man simply because he was beautiful. He didn't understand his behavior, but he knew that he was heading toward the Italian man's apartment, and he knew that we would have sex before he left that apartment. For the first time in his relationship, he felt like he was cheating. There was definitely something different about what he was doing this time. He knew it the minute that he gave Chris his cell phone number instead of the number at the house. He would keep this one a secret.

As Colin drove up to the address that Chris had given him, he didn't realize that he was about to embark on an adventure. An adventure that would affect all of their lives, and one that would change just about everything that Colin knew and loved. For him, at that moment, it was just another gay man cheating on his lover(s). He knew that he had the right as a leather top to have sex where and with whom ever he wanted it – he also knew that he was betraying the relationship, no only sexually, but emotionally as well. That was where the problem would come in.

Chapter 2

The next day, Colin sat in his office reliving the night before. He was physically present, conducting a meeting with his senior consulting staff, but his mind was going back to the night before. Chris and he made love. It wasn't the rough and tumble sex of two leather men, or even the tender sex of lovers, but the hot intense sex that occurs only once between two people, the first time they do it. Never before had Colin met such a beautiful man. Never before had vanilla sex taken him to such heights of ecstasy.

"Excuse me, Colin, but what do you think?" Martin, his administrative assistant, asked.

"I'm sorry Martin, what was the question again?"

The seven people around the table exchanged worried, knowing looks at each other. Martin cleared his throat and asked once again, "Do you think that we should take the Cleveland job? It's going to be tough going, and I'm not sure that the institution has the means to pay for the complete job."

"Well, we'll ask for one half of our total estimate up front. When that money has been used, we will start to bill them for the remainder. The usual thirty days required payment clause would be put into the initial contract. That way we limit our liability for the unpaid balance. Does that meet with your approval?"

The group seemed satisfied with what Colin thought was the obvious answer. While they finished up their discussions, he mused that his job would always be to point out the obvious. That's what his company did most, going into a situation in some health care setting, assessing the problems, and pointing out the obvious solutions to the people that hired them. It seemed like easy money to him.

When he got back into his office alone, his cell phone rang. "Hello sexy," Chris said after Colin picked up. "I really enjoyed myself last night. I hope that it wasn't just a one time thing with you."

"Well, usually I don't do these things, but for such a beautiful Italian boy like yourself, I think that I don't have any other option than to at least try to do it again. I'm definitely under your spell."

"Good then. Take me to dinner tonight."

Without thinking of the consequences or the required excuses, Colin agreed. Al never cared if Colin was there or not. He had become a fish out of water thanks to Derek's ambivalence toward Colin. It was fairly certain that Derek wouldn't be home either. He would either come in late and go directly to bed, or, he would be in bed when Colin got home. Either way, he didn't seem to care what Colin did one way or the other. That was how it all began, almost innocently enough, with Colin feeling rejected by the man he really loved, and Derek not caring enough to dissuade him from those feelings.

He left work early and made reservations at a rather expensive steak house in downtown Columbus. By six o'clock, he found himself knocking at the Chris' apartment.

"Hello sexy," the Italian boy said as he almost leapt at Colin.

"Hey, you're the sexy one."

"I can't even begin to tell you how much fun I had last night. Who would have thought that an older man could do that to me," Chris replied, smiling.

It was a smile that Colin couldn't interpret. He didn't know if Chris was really joking around, being coy, or terribly self-assured. Well, he was Italian. "I had a great time as well."

"Where are you taking me to dinner?"

"Let's let that be a surprise. Are you ready?"

Without further ado, the two men turned and, within a few minutes, were seated at a rather staid steak house in the middle of Columbus. It started out with a cocktail, followed by a great meal; the wine flowed freely during the dinner. As they stared into each other's eyes over coffee and cognac, Colin realized that he needed to sober up. Chris' apartment wasn't terribly far away, and the walk would do them both good.

When they arrived at the door, Colin honestly thought that

he would simply kiss the boy goodbye and be on his merry way. Chris had other ideas. When Colin closed his eyes and leaned in for a kiss, Chris grabbed him by the collar and pulled him into the apartment.

"Hey! Watch out, you could hurt someone?"

"And I bet you would like that," Chris replied.

Colin smiled at the boy. Little did he know the stone that he had uncovered. They made love again that night. Tender, quiet love. And, when it was over, Colin got up and made his excuses.

"Why do you have to go home? Do you have a wife?"

"No, not a wife, but two husbands!"

Chris, at first, started to laugh, and then looked puzzled.

"Well, it's a little complicated. I'm into leather, and, in that community, definitions of relationships often get a little murky. For years, I had a partner who was also my submissive. At some point, we invited a third into our relationship. Derek, Al, and I have formed a loving unit. We live together with a couple who rents from us and lives on our third floor."

Chris now stood up and assumed a position that Colin could only deduce as confrontational. "Are they part of your unique family as well?"

"Part? Yes. But not an integral part."

"And what is that supposed to mean?"

"We have meals together often. We share our experiences, and yes, sometimes we share each other."

Chris stared intently into Colin's eyes. The silence in the room became almost oppressive. After what seemed to be an eternity, Chris, in what could only be described as a low growl, spoke, "Well. Interesting arrangement you have there. I mean, I have never heard of such a thing. You say you're involved in leather, so I assume that one or the other of you beats up on the others. I may be young, but I've been around. I guess that I fell for the charms of a slime ball who's working out his midlife crisis in a very bad way. Perhaps you should leave."

The words stung. They stung because Colin was particularly sensitive about his age, and because they were coming from someone who was much younger, and much more attractive. He didn't want to explain, he simply wanted to go somewhere and lick his wounds. He turned and walked back to the restaurant where he left his car. He was definitely sober enough to drive himself home.

When he entered his house, it was totally dark except for the faint light about the cabinets in the kitchen. He walked into the room and found Derek sitting at the table, crying.

"Hey, what's the matter, little one?"

"Oh Colin, I wish you didn't find me here. Where have you been?"

"No where that matters. Come on, tell me what's wrong?"

"Nothing really, and everything really. I know that I should be happy. A great house, lots of people around, a nice city, but its very hard for me. I think that I'm having a crisis of faith or something. It's just that Christianity seems to make heterosexuality a litmus test for faith. Not just the born again people like that Rev. Mark Marjoram, but the Episcopal Church and even my old friend, who is now my bishop. "

"Are you sure that it's not a crisis of faith about me?"

Derek began to laugh. "No, Colin, its not always about you. This one is the real thing. About God and the Church and me being a priest."

"I always told you that you could be anything you wanted to be."

"That's just it, I don't know what I want to be, and I've been so miserable to everyone, I can't even stand myself anymore."

"Well, lets go to bed, little one. We all forgive you. Try to just curl up with us tonight and be a little friendly. We don't bite…often. We'll work it all out, don't worry, we have all the time in the world."

Colin put his arm around Derek, kissed him lightly, and led him up the stairs to their room. They both undressed and slid into bed beside a sleeping Al. Colin was in the middle, with his arm over Derek. Al unconsciously responded to their presence by rolling over and putting his arm over Colin. They all slept more soundly that night than they had in a long time.

Chapter 3

While the boys slept, somewhere in the wilds of West Virginia, a group of somewhat over-the-hill leather men met in a cabin by a mountain stream. There were a total of five of them; each of them dressed meticulously in leather. In the next room, a naked boy of about twenty-two was strung up to a St. Andrew's cross, his eyes blindfolded and his mouth taped shut.

"Well, we finally get together again. The few of us that remain in this club," said the apparent leader.

"Oh Joseph, you know that there are a lot of us left in the club. Only two men have been put in jail. And they aren't going to be there for a long time. After all, who knows if that Arab boy died because of a scene gone bad," a man named Dave said.

"True, but we can't have our club members all going to jail because of 'a scene gone bad'. There are too many coincidences in this club. What with Ben being in jail along with that stupid Brandy. Why did we trust *him*?"

"We've made mistakes Joseph, that's true, but there still is a very large following of us. After all, we are international. It's only a few of us."

"Dave, I know that. But we have to be careful. Brandy was just a weird person. Ben was obsessed with revenge against Colin and his boy toy, Billy. It's not like we want to take over the world, but you have to admit, the state of leather in the world leaves a lot to be desired."

"I don't know Joseph, maybe we hardcore ones are wrong. After all, look at Colin. He lives with a house full of beautiful men. He's rich, and he still has a lot of respect in the leather community."

"I'll hand you that. But he doesn't have the edge that we have. Boys don't come to him to be neutered or tortured like we do in this club. And, he's ruining that Daniel. Daniel had potential, but then Colin got to him and he stopped short."

One of the other men, John, came over and interrupted the intense conversation. "Hey, are we going to play with that thing in the other room, or just sit here and talk all night?"

"Get the other men, we're ready."

The five of them got up and went into the other room. It wasn't readily apparent whether the boy on the cross was joyfully awaiting them or dreading what they were about to do. Joseph started by picking up a single tail whip and giving the man about twenty lashes. One of the men then took a ball stretcher and secured it tightly around the young man's testicles. He attached a very heavy weight. Someone else put nipple clamps and hung another weight from the chain dangling between the two clamps. Clothespins were put in various places around the boy's groin.

John roughly pulled the tape off of the boy's mouth causing him to cry out. Dave picked up a flogger and started to work on the boy's back that was already cut open and bruised by the single tail that Joseph had used on him.

Two of the men drifted off from the center of the room and started blowing each other. Joseph and Dave turned to John and took his pants off, one of them fucking his ass while the other fed him his cock. The boy hung there. He wasn't able to watch the sex that was going on, he was facing the wall, still blindfolded.

It seemed to take forever for these guys to reach a climax. Joseph came first, then Dave. At that point, everyone else simply stopped what they were doing and joined the group once more. They turned their attention to the boy. His blindfold was removed, and he was taken down from the cross. All of the clamps and weights were finally removed.

"Bend over boy," Joseph growled.

The boy bent over, and Joseph picked up a butt plug. It was huge. He spit on it and shoved it in the boy's ass. "Clean up this room, pig."

"Yes sir," the boy replied in a voice so soft that it was hard to hear.

The five men all left the room for the boy to clean up the mess that they had made. When he was finished, he cleaned the toys, put them back on the shelves where they were stored and went over to a small mattress in the corner. It was here that he finally lay down and pulled a thin cover over himself, the butt plug still securely in his ass.

In the other room, the five older men sat around discussing old times and playing cards. It was clear from their actions that they preferred the company of each other to the boy in the other room. Most men in their fifties and sixties would jump at the chance to spend the night with a twenty something boy. Most men that age would have turned their sexual attention to him instead of each other. Had anyone viewed the scene, it would have been readily apparent to him that the boy was just there for inspiration. They only wanted to use him, not necessarily have sex with him.

The next morning, the five men dressed and took their few belongings out to their cars. They said their goodbyes and left the cabin in the woods. When they were finally out of sight, the boy got up and removed the butt plug. He took a long, hot shower and went into the kitchen and made himself something to eat. He sat there, staring out the window. As with everything else over the past two days, it wasn't apparent if he was satisfied, disgusted, or just in a state of shock.

After a long reflection, he cleaned up the kitchen, packed his bags, locked the door and went out to get into his car. He turned on the ignition and backed out of the area where he had parked. It wasn't long before he was driving down the highway, making the turn to head toward Pittsburgh. At some point, he put on the radio and mindlessly drove.

When he arrived at his house, he entered into the lush surroundings, picked up his mail, listened to the messages on his answering service, and started to unpack. He picked up the leather vest from his bag and hung it in his closet. The dark purple Maltese cross on the back of the vest signifying his membership in the Dark Knights of St. Germaine, was hung in the closet, separately from all of the rest of the leather. The cross was so dark that it was almost imperceptible. When he looked at it hanging there, he seemed content, closed the closet door and went on with his life.

Chapter 4

Over the next couple of weeks, the trio in Columbus managed to reconnect with each other. Derek, always the reflective one, while not being effusive, was certainly in a much better mood than he had been for a couple of months. He, Colin and Al started having sex... real sex again, and joking around. Billy and Daniel noticed it immediately, as did Dominic.

"I'm so glad that my parents aren't breaking up anymore," Billy said as he and Colin were folding laundry in the basement.

"Who ever said that we were breaking up?"

"Well, it seemed that way for a while. You and Derek were at each other's throats and Al was just sitting around looking like he made the biggest mistake of his life."

"Any you, Billy? What were you doing during this time?"

"Waiting to get back to normal so we can all play again."

Billy knelt down in from on Colin and pulled his zipper down. "Hey, don't I need permission for you to do this?" Colin asked.

"You know that Daniel doesn't care what you and I do," said Billy, and then proceeded to swallow Colin's eight inches. It didn't take long for Colin to reach that point of no return. He didn't hear people coming down the steps to the basement. Just as he came all over Billy's face, Derek and Daniel entered the room. For one split second there was total silence. Then both Derek and Daniel started to laugh; Colin and Billy joined in.

"Well, its nice to see that we're all back to normal, including the little whore," joked Derek.

"I hope that you still have the stamina for me," joined Daniel.

Daniel and Derek started groping each other, while Billy changed his position and did to Daniel what he had just done to Colin. Colin watched for a minute and then returned to folding laundry. "Ah...the little family at home," he said to the wall. Within minutes, the entire exchange was over.

"Who's cooking dinner tonight?" Daniel asked.

"We're all going to Dominic's tonight; he's making spaghetti," Colin answered.

The little group, all with laundry in their arms, made their way upstairs and found Al in the kitchen. "The whole family was downstairs doing laundry, and you didn't make me help? I don't know if I should be hurt or happy that I was excused."

"Well Al, you did miss out on the blowjobs," Derek and Daniel replied in unison.

"Blow jobs and laundry? Only in this house."

"Hey Al, get ready. We're all invited to Dominic's for dinner tonight. Spaghetti," Colin injected.

"Yes Sir," Al replied and went upstairs to change his clothes.

Within a few minutes, the five of them went out the back door, crossed the yard, and knocked on Dominic's kitchen door.

"Come in," Dominic said as he greeted his guests at the door.

The house was filled with the smells of a great Italian dinner. Dominic greeted each of the men with a hug and a kiss. He noticed the change in atmosphere almost immediately. "So, it looks like we're all back to normal?" he asked.

"What is it with everyone here? I have a couple of weeks of being slightly distracted and everyone acts like I did something totally horrible," Derek answered.

"Well, I don't want to be the one to have to inform you, my pretty, but it was certainly more than a couple of weeks, and if that's what you call slightly distracted, I would hate to see it when you're in a bad mood," Billy joined in, being a little more forward than he usually was.

"Bitch whore!" was Derek's only response.

"Hey boys, let's not fight here," Colin intervened.

"Yes Sir," Derek, Al, and Billy said at the same time and burst into laughter.

Dinner that night was spectacular. Colin and Dominic served all the men. The wine flowed freely and the conversation was friendly and often funny. Near the end of the evening, as they lingered over coffee and cognac, Dominic got a far away look in his eyes. Colin noticed it immediately and put his hand on Dom's shoulder. "I know that you miss him."

"More than you will ever know."

"As bad as this sounds, I hope that I never know that kind of loss," Colin said as the rest of the men looked on.

"It doesn't sound bad. It's my fervent hope for all of you," Dominic said as he rested his head against Colin's chest. "It's not bad all of the time, and it does seem to get better every day, but I honestly think that Amin was my life mate."

"You need to move on, Dominic," Al said. "Please don't take that the wrong way, but you're too young to lock yourself in some negative space, away from everyone."

"I know. I know. Sometimes, it's just so hard. I have gone out; even have had some incredible sex, but.... I don't know."

"Sex? Sex with who?" Billy asked, causing all of the men to dissolve into laughter.

"Only you would ask as question like that at a time like this," Daniel said.

"I want to know. We have no secrets from each other," Billy responded.

Colin felt a pang of guilt—something that he rarely felt. He would have to rid himself of this feeling soon. He couldn't forget the moments that he had spent with Chris; and couldn't forget how painful were the final harsh words that they exchanged. He often thought of calling the young man, but then talked himself out of it, either because of the pain of the last encounter, or the guilt that he felt from almost emotionally betraying his somewhat less-than-conventional relationship.

"Well, if you have to know, I did meet a hot young man in the Short North about a week ago," Dominic answered.

"Now, this is good. Is it someone that I know? Did you meet him in the bookstore? What did you do?" Billy relentlessly continued his questioning.

"I don't know if you know him. I met him at the little gay bar/ restaurant that I can never remember the name of. And I don't think I have to tell you what we did."

"Why not? We tell you everything, and even invite your hot little ass into our play times," Billy continued.

"What has gotten into this boy? Don't you spank him enough Daniel?" Colin asked.

"Apparently," Daniel answered, "but I can take care of that a little later."

"And, I really hate to change the subject, but, Daniel, have you heard anything more from the Dark Knights of St. Germaine?" Dominic asked.

"No. I seriously doubt that I ever will. Of course, I don't go down dark streets without looking over my shoulder anymore. And I call Billy's cell phone every ten minutes when he's not with me, but basically, other than the terrible fear for my life and the uneasiness about having my boyfriend kidnapped... no, nothing."

Everyone laughed, uneasily. "I just don't know what I was thinking when I joined them," he continued.

"Well, don't beat yourself up about it. When I was initially looking into it, I discovered that they have a long history, and a rather noble purpose. It seems that the membership of local group in this country might be a little off," Dominic replied, trying to assuage Daniel's guilt.

"Tell us more," Billy urged.

"Well, as much as we all like to believe that we invented sex and our own little variation in leather, it has actually been around for quite some time. The uniform has changed significantly, but there have always been sadism in the world."

"Yeah, like the Marquis de Sade?" Billy injected.

"Right. In Europe, there have always been some groups that have dedicated themselves to rougher play. And, like any group of men, they formed a club dedicated to that purpose. Originally, it was restricted to nobles, or, at least people who had money. But, eventually they opened their ranks to others. There was the required long 'apprenticeship' followed by elaborate initiation ceremonies. This was coupled with absolute secrecy, primarily because, if they were found out, they would suffer consequences. I don't think that they truly harmed anyone; the play was edgy, but they had principles."

"So, this club was the model for our leather clubs here? The original old guard?" Daniel asked.

"Not really. Of course, you could probably speak about them like that, but leather in this country is much younger. And, it's associated with the wearing of leather. There are theorists who say that it happened when men came back from World War II, they liked the all male environment, and the homoeroticism of it all, and they liked the hierarchy of military life. They got motorcycles and went off on weekends by themselves. Our current history is probably a direct descendent of that. They became our old guard."

"Yeah, I've heard about this old guard all my life. My friends always want to be a part of it," Billy added.

"I didn't think that it existed, that it was a myth," Al continued.

"Well, ask Colin. A very proficient and strict Master introduced us to leather. We looked up to him and, at the time, although we didn't know the term, probably thought of him as old guard. I guess that each generation of leather men try to rewrite the book. If the men in the fifties in this country thought of themselves as leather men, they didn't know that they were the original writers of what has become the unwritten 'leather constitution'. They just played. If, on the other hand, there was a gradual development of customs and protocol, does that matter? If old guard was an evolution as opposed to an initial institution, it doesn't bother me. If the principles that Colin, Daniel, and I adhere to when we enter into that headspace we call leather, use aspects that have become known as old guard traits, does it matter if it is history or philosophy?"

"Wow, Dominic! I haven't heard you be this philosophical since our teenage years," Colin said. "But I do have to say, that the lessons that we were taught by Heinrich were so codified, that there was some system that it came from. Maybe old guard is a term that we need to rethink. Who was the old guard? Was it the leather men from the fifties in this country? Or was it the sixties? Or perhaps could it have been as late as the early seventies? All I know is that the code existed when we came along. Of course, Heinrich always said that there was a much older tradition, the European one, that added a new dimension to the whole thing. Who knows? Perhaps the only thing that America contributed was the actual uniform."

"So, what you're saying, all philosophy aside, is that this group of dark knights, for the most part, aren't the criminal element that we have experienced so far?" Derek asked.

"Right. I think that there were a few people in this country who were admitted who shouldn't have been. I think that they had problems, whatever they were. I think that the whole thing with the surgeon in Pittsburgh was a mistake and that they panicked and we've seen the result of what has happened," Dominic continued.

"So, should we think that Billy is safe now? And that we all aren't marked for some kind of lesson from this group?" Derek asked.

"That I don't know, but I do know that until the bad element is out of this group, we have to be a little more careful around here."

"I agree with my cousin. If there is a bad element in that club, it will work to seek whatever it wants or it will destroy itself doing it. We should be careful. But, for right now, I think that we've eaten too much, drank too much, and stayed up way too late talking, it's after two in the morning," said Colin.

"It's just that it feels so good being a cohesive group again," Al added.

"Yeah, I know, I've been giving everyone grief. I'm sorry, just bear with me," Derek continued. "It will get better, and I'm sorry to put you through this so early in the relationship for you, Al," Derek said as he put his arm around his counterpart in the family.

"Well, let's go. Dominic, if you want company in bed, you can come over and sleep with us. But I doubt that there will be any sex," Colin offered.

"I think that I will take you up on that. You're all right, I've been spending too much time alone." Dominic got up, threw all the glasses and plates in the kitchen sink, turned off the lights, got his keys and walked out with the other five men. Within minutes of undressing and getting into bed, the four men were sound asleep. That kind of intimacy only comes when everyone is deeply in love with each other.

Billy and Daniel were on their floor. Billy wanting sex, but too tired to do anything about it. He felt safe and warm cuddled in Daniel's arms. For that night, the six men in the house looked like they didn't have a care in the world.

Chapter 5

Colin had a meeting the next morning. After that, he had a lunch date with the CEO of a major medical center back in Pittsburgh, Mary Rose Grabnicki; a legend in her own right. While Colin's fucks in the gay world were indeed legendary, Mary Rose was known for her out front sexuality, an uncommon trait in a straight woman. Colin sat through the morning meeting with a slight hangover and a noticeable lack of sufficient sleep. When it was over, he slipped out of the office and made his way to the restaurant that Mary Rose had picked.

When he arrived, she was seated at a prime table, one that commanded a view of the whole room *and* the entrance. She had a way of getting the prime spot, no matter what the venue was. As Colin went up to the host, she waved discreetly to him. He went over and they embraced. They had worked together off and on for several years, and were truly friends. If Colin were a bit younger, Mary Rose would have made the perfect fag hag... pretty, well dressed, fun, and irreverent. In many ways, Colin thought that Mary Rose was a gay man trapped in a straight women's body. She was intelligent, but had a humorous ability to misuse words that often changed the entire meaning of what she was trying to convey.

"Colin, dear, how nice of you to meet me," Mary Rose said as she sat back down.

"It's always a pleasure to see you. I thought that my leaving Pittsburgh would be the last that I saw any of the professional colleagues I had there."

"What have you been up to? I need to know everything – work, your company, your love life... everything."

Colin went over everything that he felt Mary Rose could handle. Gay men, when talking with anyone, fag hags included, must edit what they are saying. He went over his work here in

Columbus, the founding of his company and its progress. He let her know about his three way relationship and the friends that lived upstairs, his cousin, and now, old friends moving very close to his house. It didn't take long for him to bring her up to date; Colin was very efficient at summarizing complex issues and concepts in a few words. He finished up, then asked, "Any you? What have you been up to? And not professionally."

"Well, since my last divorce, I haven't wanted a new man. I've been dating a bit."

"Dating anyone interesting?"

"Well yes. There have been a few, including a world famous surgeon."

"World famous? Aren't they all old or dead?"

"No, world famous, as in right now, Colin. He is so incredibly hot and very good in bed."

"Are you dating a younger man?" Colin asked. Mary Rose, although a little older than Colin, looked much younger. And since she had what Colin referred to her front-end realignment, a breast job, she looked downright perky.

"No, he's a little older. Gray hair. That turns me on. We do everything in bed. It's a regular Kama-Sumatra, and I really should get that book."

Colin started laughing. Mary Rose was perplexed, "What are you laughing about? Straight people can have good sex."

"Well, I agree with you, although I can't imagine what you people do in bed. But, my dear, Sumatra is a type of coffee, or the place it came from. I believe that you are referring to the Kama Sutra; that's the book that details sexual positions."

Mary Rose laughed out loud. One of her most endearing characteristics was her ability to laugh at herself. Very strong, intelligent, and accomplished women often couldn't do that. Her laughter was contagious, and soon, Colin joined her laughing like school children over a bad joke. When he composed himself, Colin continued, "So, you're dating this guy. Where is it going? I hope that you at least get a car out of the deal."

"It's not going anywhere Colin, he's married."

"Married? So, how do you date in a little city like Pittsburgh?"

"He calls me and we have sex."

Colin started laughing again. "Well, in the gay community, we call that fucking."

"Whatever, it works for me."

"Did you at least get a car?"

"No," she replied. "It's all very *Sex in the City*. You know, I have a cosmopolitan, buy some Milanos, and have sex with a very powerful man."

"Milanos? The cookies?"

"No silly. The shoes."

Even Colin couldn't contain himself this time. He laughed so hard that he thought for a minute he wouldn't be able to breath. By now, the couple had become quite the spectacle in the restaurant. When he finally got a hold of himself, he said, "Mary Rose, in the series, *Sex in the City*, Carrie buys Manolo's, I believe that it's the name of the designer. Milanos, my dear, are cookies."

This time, there was no restraint to their laughter. They laughed long and loudly and people around them started to smile and giggle, simply because of how infectious it was to have two attractive people sitting there, dissolved in laughter. When they finally managed to compose themselves, Mary Rose looked up and said, "I haven't had this much fun since you left Pittsburgh. Which brings me to the purpose of my coming to Columbus. I need an administrator back in Pittsburgh, and, I was wondering, are you ready to come back?"

"Let me get this straight. My lover is an HIV positive Episcopal priest. We have a three-way marriage with a man who left the Catholic priesthood. We were involved with a man who was murdered by a psychopathic nut case in an S/M scene, and you think that I'm the person for a public job like an administrative position?"

"Sure, why not?" she replied.

"Have you brought this up to the board?" he asked.

"Not yet, I wanted to know if you were interested."

"Well, that would depend... like on salary. But, even if the salary is great, I doubt that the board would want *the* notorious homosexual in that position."

"Colin, I don't know how your business is doing, but this is six figures—and certainly not just six figures."

"Well, when you put it that way, let's just say that I would consider it. Of course I have to talk to my spouses. But, while we're on the subject, if that doesn't work out for us, I was thinking of recruiting you for my consulting company. We're doing really well. You would love it. You go in, you look around a hospital or a practice. You tell them what they are doing wrong and they pay you well for it."

"How well?" she asked.

"Tell you what. You go back to your board. I'll go to my staff, and we can meet again with proposals for each other."

"Deal."

Lunch had taken about four hours. Colin, still hung over and sleepy from the night before, needed to get home, get out of his tie and just veg out for a while. They said their goodbyes and walked out to their respective cars. Colin, who usually didn't feel anything from interactions with straight people, was pleasantly happy about the few hours he spent with his old friend. It *would* be fun to work with her again.

Chapter 6

Derek's day was typical of an Episcopal priest. He visited the sick, counseled those that were in crisis, and attended meetings. The Episcopal Church seemed to be all about meetings. Late in the afternoon, the phone rang. "Hello, St. Peter's," Derek answered.

"Hello Derek, this is Millicent."

"Hey, to what do I owe the honor of having my bishop call me?" Derek asked. "Or, is this a not pleasant call from my boss?"

"Well Derek, it's a little of both. How have you been?"

"I'm doing OK, Mill. You know what its like. You do the same stuff over and over; sometimes you just need a jump-start. The parish seems to be doing OK. Colin and Al are great; the house is wonderful. I have nothing to complain about. And you?"

"I'm doing just fine."

"I imagine that was the pleasant part of the conversation, what's the problem, Bishop?" Derek asked.

"Well, as you know, we're a church in crisis, right now, Derek. It all has to do with homosexuality. And, you're regularly performing blessing services for same sex couples at St. Peter's. I'm getting complaints."

"Millicent, I'm simply praying over them. They are aware that it is not the sacrament of matrimony. I'm being a representative of the church to witness their commitment to each other and to offer the only thing that we have to offer, our prayerful support."

"That's just the problem, Derek. We've discussed this before. It puts the Church, and I'm using Church with a capital C, out there for everyone to challenge what we truly believe."

"Millicent, isn't that what Jesus did? He challenged how we believe, what we believe, how we act toward each other. There were outcasts among his followers. Mary Magdalene was given a position of honor at a time when women were not even considered second class citizens, they were chattel."

"Derek, I don't want to discuss theology with you right now. Not only have there been complaints from Episcopalians, but I'm getting them from other religious leaders, the Reverend Mark Marjoram particularly."

"Oh, come on Millicent, you can't seriously expect me to react to what *he* says, can you?"

"Perhaps not. But I can expect you to react to what I say. Stop the blessings."

"Fine. Good bye Bishop."

The call ended abruptly. Derek couldn't believe this. Of all things for people to worry about, for heaven's sake, couldn't the Christian community survive with a few people who wished to remain in the fold and be a little different? He had more to do that day, but just closed up shop and went home. Al was at the kitchen table, cooking dinner and studying his psychology textbook.

"Hey there sexy," he greeted Derek.

"Hi," was Derek's only response.

"Oh no, not again. You're not going to get all prissy again are you? What happened?"

"Not much—just a fight with my bishop."

"Those are to be expected. Be glad you're not Catholic. They would have you in a monastery, repenting your sins, or, worse yet, sent to Utah to minister to some miniscule parish. What was the fight about?"

"Gay rights. Let's not talk about it. You're right, it will just get me all mad, all over again."

"Have you heard from Colin? I haven't, and that's a little unusual."

"He's having lunch with some colleague from Pittsburgh.... Mary something."

"Mary Rose, the whore of Babylon?"

"What? Who?" Al asked.

"She's a great woman. Funny, pretty, messed up like we are all messed up, but has sense enough to be able to laugh about it. She generally puts Colin in a good mood, unless he has to answer to her."

They heard Colin's jeep drive up and Finocchio started

barking. Billy came bounding down the back stairs from the third floor. "You and the dog act alike when he comes home," Al joked.

"I haven't seen Colin all day. What's for dinner?" the young boy asked.

Derek and Al both started laughing. Not only did he respond to Colin's car, just like the dog, he also was constantly looking for food... just like the dog. Colin entered the room with Finocchio following behind him. Billy jumped up and kissed him, right on the mouth.

"Hey, he's my husband," Derek yelled.

"And mine too," Al joined in.

"We get him first," they said in unison.

"Hey guys, wait a minute, there's enough of me to go around," Colin said, eating up the thought of three hot men lined up to kiss him. Maybe those Mormons had something going for them.

Dinner that night was fun. All five of the men from the house, along with Dominic, enjoyed Al's dinner. It wasn't a gourmet dinner, just meatloaf, rice and vegetables, but it was the company that kept everyone in good spirits. Colin regaled them with Mary Rose's meeting and Derek voiced his concerns with Millicent. After dinner, as Derek and Al cleaned up, Dominic excused himself quickly. He had a date. Billy tried to get him to tell him who it was, but Dominic wouldn't. Colin and Daniel decided to walk Finocchio.

When the two Masters were safely out the door, Derek, Al, and Billy started to conspire. "We need a night in the basement," Derek stated.

"You got that right," Al said, putting the last of the washed and dried pots away.

"You up for it, Billy?" Derek asked.

"Are you kidding? Do we have enough time to get ready?"

"When those two go out they are usually gone for half an hour, hurry up. Get the gear laid out for them, get something on, and get prepared. The first one ready, goes to the basement and sets up the dungeon," Al barked orders which betrayed his intense anticipation to get back to basics in the house.

It didn't take the men long to prepare. Most had already showered, and taken care of any other personal hygiene tasks that would be required. Colin's leather was laid out on his bed, as was

Daniel's. Each Master was given a simple written request: 'If it would please you, join us in the basement.'

When they arrived back at the house, Colin called out for someone. No one answered. Daniel did the same thing. For a brief second, there was a feeling of dread—that something had happened while they were gone. Everything looked in order, so they decided to go upstairs and see where their lovers were.

On the way up, both men looked into Colin's room. There was his leather, and the note. "Go upstairs, it appears we have duties to do, Daniel," Colin said. "Let's both take showers first; we can keep them guessing down there if we're going to come or not."

"You can be such a sadist at times, Colin," Daniel teased.

It didn't take them long. They were fresh, in leather, and ready to play. They stopped in the library and had a drink before going downstairs. "Should we plan what we're going to do?" Daniel asked.

"Let's just let the scene take us to where ever it does."

When they walked into the basement, they could see the glow of candlelight in the back room. They walked slowly to the door. It was ajar. Daniel kicked it open and stepped aside as Colin walked in. There, in the center of the dungeon, the three slave boys were kneeling. Each attired in the same way; leather collars, harnesses, and boots; nothing else.

There were candelabras with massive candles in them. In the back room, a black light illuminated a leather poster of two men engaged in an intimate pose. In the background, interesting music was playing—nothing that would grab anyone's attention, just something that would set the dark mood.

Colin walked over to Al. He grabbed him by the collar. Since both Masters had chaps on with only a jock strap underneath, there was easy access. Al licked the cloth holding his Master's cock and balls. Derek knelt silently, eyes down, waiting for instructions. While Al paid attention to Colin's still sheathed cock, Daniel was making Billy do the same to him. Colin pulled his jock down and plunged his cock deep into Al's mouth.

"Take it all, bitch," he growled. "You, other slave...eat my ass."

Derek gladly crawled over and started to lick Colin's ass

while Al sucked his cock. Colin thought that he was going to cum immediately, but he held off. He and Daniel were standing, side-by-side now, with Billy going after Daniel's cock like there was no tomorrow. Colin reached over and pulled Daniel's head toward him. The two men kissed deeply—each working hard to restrain themselves; it was too early in the scene for them to climax.

After a while, Colin looked over at Daniel and indicated that Billy should be put up on the cross. "Get up, boy," Daniel barked. Colin extracted his cock from Al and helped Daniel put Billy up on the cross. Daniel picked up a flogger and lightly began to flog his lover. At first, it was gentle, but within minutes, he was wailing away at Billy's back. Colin was behind him, gently rubbing his cock against Daniel's butt cheeks. Al and Derek knelt on the floor, waiting for instructions, cocks standing at attention. Both Al and Derek wanted to be flogged, but Colin knew that they hadn't been for a while. It would only have caused the scene to end too quickly. Billy's cock was dripping while he was on the cross.

Without a word, Colin turned and looked at Derek, "Get into that sling, bitch." Derek almost ran to the sling. "You, come with me," he said to Al. Colin was at the foot of the sling, putting a well-greased dildo into Derek's ass. Derek was in ecstasy. As he reached for a condom, he got Daniel's attention. Daniel knew exactly what to do. He undid the restraints holding Billy to the cross. As Colin pulled out the dildo and replaced it with his cock, plowing it deep into Derek's ass, Al began to lick his Master's ass. Daniel stood at the head of the sling and made Derek suck his cock while Billy rimmed him. With all that going on, the two Masters knew that it wouldn't be long before they were ready.

"Get yourselves off boys," Colin instructed. The three of them began to play with their cocks. It was Colin who came first, followed by Daniel. Within seconds all three boys climaxed as well.

No one said a word. No one moved for several minutes. All of them seemed to be in another place. After several minutes, Daniel let out a long sigh, "Wow! I forgot how good this could be."

"I agree with you there Dan, we need to do this more often," Colin answered. "Boys, go get yourselves cleaned up and straighten up the dungeon." The two Masters walked out. They went upstairs to Colin's bathroom to shower. They showered together, groping each other, kissing, and washing each other. The three boys showered downstairs and cleaned up the dungeon, taking care to make sure that the candles were all out, the floors cleaned up, the toys put away. They came upstairs and found Colin and Daniel on the bed, making out like teenagers. Billy came over and Daniel got up, took him by the hand and led him upstairs. Derek and Al slid in beside their lover and Master. He put his arms around them both. All the men, on both floors were soon asleep—peacefully asleep. It had been a while since it had last happened. All of them knew that it had to happen more frequently.

Chapter 7

Several days later, Colin was walking Finocchio when he ran into his old friend Lee, and his lover, Michael, "Hey, have you guys settled in yet?"

Lee and Michael came over and embraced Lee's old friend, "Just about. We've both decided that we will never move again." Finocchio sniffed around the two men, making sure that they were acceptable.

"How come neither of you have called me since you came to town?" Colin asked.

"Well, we've been kind of busy, and tired. Besides, you were just in New Orleans with Lee," Michael responded.

"We've been meaning to call, but, first its one thing, and then another. I did see Dominic the other day, and I think Billy, once. Haven't seen Derek," Lee added.

"And don't forget Al or Daniel," Colin joked.

"How many people do you have living there anyway?" Michael asked.

"Long story, but Dominic lives next to you. We'll have to have you over for dinner sometime soon. Right now, I have to walk the beast. Take care guys, and keep in touch."

For some reason that night, Colin took Finocchio for a long walk. It was almost an hour later when he was coming up the sidewalk that he noticed Dominic getting out of his car in the driveway between the houses. At first, Colin thought that he would sneak up on his cousin and surprise him. As he got closer, he realized that Dominic was not alone. Chris, the beautiful Italian boy, was standing in the driveway, waiting for Dominic to let him into his house.

Colin felt a rush of emotions...guilt, jealousy, anxiety, and passion. He wondered if this was the man that Dominic was referring to the last time he made dinner for the clan.

Neither Chris nor Dominic noticed Colin lurking around the tree on the other side of the driveway. After they went into the house, Colin took Finocchio home.

Once inside the house, Chris grabbed Dominic and kissed him passionately. "You better watch out man, I might be falling for you," the young Italian man said.

"And that would be bad, because?" Dominic asked.

"Do you think that you could handle a young stud like me?"

"Oh, I think I could."

Dominic led the younger man upstairs to the bedroom. Once he had him there, he slowly kissed him on the mouth while grabbing for his cock. Chris's hair was so thick and black; it was so terribly sexy. Dominic's own hair was just as black and thick, but with a tinge of gray at the temples, and much shorter.

"I want you to fuck me tonight," Chris pleaded.

"Well then, I think that you will get your wish."

Dominic pushed Chris to the bed; he pulled off his shoes and socks and undid his belt. He pulled the boy's pants down with one yank. Chris never wore underwear. As he did this, Chris pulled his shirt above his head and laid there, flat on his back, staring at Dominic.

Dominic didn't even undress. He undid his belt and let his pants fall to the floor. He reached to the bedside table, pulled out a condom and some lube, put Chris's legs over his shoulders and fucked the boy. At first it wasn't rough or fast, but slow and deliberate. Dominic pulled his nine inch cock almost all the way out and then slowly slid it back into Chris's hole. For his part, Chris seemed to be in ecstasy. As time went on, Dominic stepped up the pace and eventually was pounding Chris's ass quickly and roughly. As Dominic came, Chris grabbed his own cock and came – spraying Dominic as he screamed in pleasure. Chris's cum went right into Dominic's mouth. He swallowed it, licked his lips, pulled out his cock and leaned over and kissed the boy softly on the mouth.

Meanwhile, next door, Colin went upstairs to find Al and Derek in bed, curled around each other watching a gay movie on television. He smiled at the tableau before him, undressed completely and walked over to be serviced by both men. Derek sucked his cock while he and Al kissed passionately. When Colin finally came, he commanded the two boys, “You two don’t get to cum tonight.” Colin left the room to get a shower and the two boys simply went back to what they were doing. When the movie was over, Colin slid into bed beside his two lovers.

“So, tell me about your day,” he said, kissing them both on the head.

“Well, I had an exam. It seems that I’ll never be done with school. I thought that eight years was enough—now I’m doing more,” Al sighed.

“And I dealt with crazy bishops, crazy Protestant evangelical ministers and whiney church people all day. And you, what happened in your day?” Derek chided.

“The usual.”

“Does that mean hot sex for breakfast, sexual tension at lunch, a nooner on campus, then a quickie fuck during the dog walk and finally us to take the final load?” Al joked.

As Colin picked up a pillow and began beating Al, and then Derek, over the head, they all started laughing. “But seriously Derek, is life getting any easier for you? You can quit, you know.”

“I know. It’s not just an easier thing. It’s a life-altering thing as well. I’ve identified my adult self as a priest. I might not know who I am.”

“Me too – but I’ve taken the plunge,” Al added.

“Well, I understand that. But remember. As a leather bottom your first identity is as a leather bottom…a slave…someone who serves…at the will and pleasure of another man, you Master. I think that we’ve gotten away from that. We have all forgotten our identity in this relationship. That happens. But now, we have to get back on track.”

“While we’re doing that, I have a couple of questions,” Al said.

“Yes?” Colin asked.

“Dominic talked about a man, Heinrich, that introduced the both of you into the leather world. You’ve never talked about him. Derek, do you know anything about this guy?”

“A little, Al,” Derek answered, “But I could always learn more about him.”

“I’ll tell you what, we will discuss that another day, when it’s not so late. Let's get to bed." Colin settled into the bed and snuggled with Derek and Al. Derek reached over an turned off the bedside light.

Upstairs, after an intense encounter with Daniel, Billy looked out the window. There, below in the driveway that separated the two houses, he saw Dominic and Chris open the door and get into the car. Dominic was taking Chris home. "Hey, I think I've finally seen Dominic's mystery man. He's cute."

"How do you know from three floors up and in the dark?" Daniel asked.

"I can see cute a mile away in dense fog, Daniel."

Dominic took Chris back to his apartment and dropped him off. They shared a passionate kiss before Chris left the car and went inside. On the way back home, Dominic stopped at a local bar for a drink. He had that permanent smile plastered on his face that only occurs to men after a very fulfilling evening. He sat down at the table. It wasn't long before the cute waiter came over and asked, "Can I get you anything, sir?"

"Yeah, a nice stiff bourbon and water."

"I'm sure you can make anything stiff, sir," the waiter replied and went off to get the drink.

As Dominic sat there, finishing his drink, an older, weathered man came up to the table and sat down. "I hate to be so forward, but haven't I seen you around the leather community?" he asked.

"Yeah. I'm involved. I can't place you though. Was it MAL, IML, or our local leather watering hole?"

"I'm not so sure either. I belong to a leather club, perhaps it was at a party somewhere."

"Well, I do kind of belong to a leather club, but it's not from around here, and I'm only peripherally involved," Dominic answered mindlessly.

"I'm sure that I've seen you. Out in the woods..."

A cold shudder went down Dominic's spine. He didn't recognize the man, and he realized that there were plenty of men in the Knights of St. Germaine who were not particularly sinister. He looked closely at the man, memorizing his face. "Well, I'm just not sure. But, if its something that I'm into, I'm sure that we'll see each other again. If you will excuse me, it's been a long day, and

I really should be going home." Dominic smiled, left money for the waiter, got up and left. When he got home that night, he patrolled the perimeter of the two houses; just to be sure everything was in order.

Chapter 8

The next morning, Colin was in his office early, even before Martin arrived. The phone rang and he picked it up, "Morgan Healthcare Consulting."

"Wow! I didn't expect to get the president on the phone."

Colin recognized Mary Rose immediately. "Hey, how have you been? I had a great time the other day."

"So did I, and I'm calling about my initial offer…I spoke to the board. Your professional reputation eclipses your personal issues. They think that you are talented and smart enough for the job and they would like us to proceed with our negotiations. We're starting out with an annual salary of $250,000. Of course, the benefits package will make that total compensation much higher. What do you think?"

Colin was dumbfounded. A quarter of a million dollars to work at a prestigious institution was, indeed, a great deal. His company, which could offer him probably just as much money over time, required more work. He paused before he answered, "Mary Rose, do we have a time frame here. I mean, do you need an answer immediately?"

"Colin, this is the initial stage of this whole thing. We are going to proceed slowly. If you make the decision to come aboard, we want you, and your family, to be happy with it. Let's say that the offer has been made. You are thinking about it. I'm going to give you a couple of weeks and then we will talk again. At that time I expect you to come back with a counter offer and we go from there."

"You really want me to ask for more money?" he said, laughing.

"Well, asking never hurts. Look, sorry to drop this on you and bolt, but I have an early meeting I got to get to."

The two old friends said goodbye, leaving Colin sitting there with a huge decision to make. But, in the meantime, he had a company to run, a realization made concrete by the arrival of Martin, his assistant. They went over the day's business and Colin spent the morning doing paperwork. He loved paperwork. He should have been an accountant—spend hours doing a report and keep his interaction with people and the real world at a minimum.

The office of Morgan Healthcare Consulting was just off the OSU campus. Colin had already arranged to meet Al for lunch. As it neared noon, he told Martin that he would be out of the office for a few hours and made the short walk over to the campus, standing in front of the library, waiting for Al to arrive. Michael, Lee's lover, was there, grading papers on a bench.

"Hey Michael, this is a pleasant surprise," Colin said as he sat down on the bench with Michael.

"Hey Colin, this is. What are you doing on campus."

"Al, the second lover, and I don't think that you've met him; he's a grad student here in psychology/counseling. We're meeting for lunch."

"How is it, having two lovers?"

"Sometimes it's the greatest thing in the world. Other times, it is like work. Overall, it's mostly great. But remember, we're into leather, so there is a whole different dynamic going on here."

"I think that Lee envies you," Michael said.

"Is that why he's been so distant lately?"

"You know, I've talked to him about it, and begged him to pay more attention to your friendship. The move has been hard on him. He loved Philadelphia, and didn't want to move. He has trouble making new friends."

"And apparently, keeping the old," Colin said.

Just then Colin felt a hand on his shoulder. He turned around and discovered Al. "Hey, how's your day. This is a friend of mine, Michael. His lover Lee and I are really old friends. They live right up the street from us."

"Hi Michael, nice to meet you," Al said, extending his hand.

"Hi Al, likewise."

After a few minutes of small talk, Colin and Al left Michael to finish grading his papers. They walked for about fifteen minutes, commenting on the unseasonably warm December weather, the boys, and Columbus in general. It wasn't long before they were established in a nice quiet booth at a restaurant right on the grounds of the campus.

"So, how are your classes?" Colin asked while sipping iced tea.

"The classes are relatively easy, but I might be tired of being in school."

"I totally understand that feeling, but its not forever. You'll be done sooner than you think. And then, you begin a new career."

"Yes, Sir, that really is what I'm looking forward to, I'm beginning to feel like a child in this relationship. Not contributing much; living off of you and Derek."

"I don't see it that way. You contribute a lot. Just because it isn't money doesn't make the contribution less valid. And perhaps, at this point, you should feel like a child in this relationship. You're still learning; and there's a lot to learn."

"That's just it, Sir, every time that I think that I have a handle on what we're doing, I find that there's even more to learn. And I'm a little upset about this whole Dark Knights thing that Billy is somehow involved in."

"Wait a second," Colin interrupted. "Billy isn't involved with that group. And the group, as a whole, might be an innocuous entity. However, there must be a bad element in it that is somehow fascinated with Billy, and, consequently, with us. In all my years in leather, this is the first time that I've been aware of a concerted effort on the part of members of our community to go after someone. It's totally bizarre."

"I know," Al said as he continued to pick around his Cobb salad.

"Is everything else all right?" Colin asked.

"Oh! Of course! Well...there for a while, when Derek was being a little whatever, it was kind of tense. I thought that I caused it."

"Al, wipe that thought completely out of your head. Over the years, there have been times when I was exactly in the same position...thinking that I had done something to cause Derek to be cold and aloof. It's just his personality. I think that it comes from being super intelligent and reflective. And, he's had to live with HIV most of his adult life."

"I know. It's just..." Al faltered for words.

"You're a pleaser," Colin finished. "That's apparent. And the one thing that a pleaser cannot stand is the inability to please someone. Don't worry too much about Derek. He just needs coddling sometime. And sometime he needs to be left alone. And sometimes he needs punishment."

Al started laughing and the two men finished their lunches. Afterward, as they were walking back to the campus, Colin stopped and turned to Al. "I've had a great idea. It will be getting cold soon... I hope. This mild December is driving me crazy. We all tend to nest during the winter months. Here's my idea. We all go to MAL in January. Dominic and I go off afterwards for some quality time. You and Derek go off and bond. Have sex with each other, without me there. And then, we all meet up, finish the holiday with a quick trip to Amsterdam and some hot European sex."

"Sex with Derek without you?" Al asked incredulously.

"Yeah, I think that it would be good. As long as the two of you don't decide to kick me out and set up housekeeping without me."

"Oh yeah Sir, two bottoms in a relationship without a resident top. That would go over really well."

"Well, it might be a tad more bitchy. But when we come back, refreshed, and, at the same time, exhausted, we can talk about the direction that our little family will be taking," Colin said as he embraced his lover.

"Will it just be you, me, Derek, and Dominic?" Al asked.

"Well, we can talk to Daniel and Billy. Perhaps they would want to do the MAL thing, go off by themselves, and then join us for our trip to the leather capital of the world."

"You know, I've never been to Amsterdam," Al added.

"Well then, you're in for a treat. You get Derek on the phone today and tell him of our plans. I'll call Daniel and have him break the news to Billy; then I'll call Dominic. A nice three week holiday in January will be fun."

"I think I might miss you when you go off with Dominic," Al added, looking a little forlorn.

"It will only be for a few days. Trust me, I'm sure that there are times when you wish I would go away for a little while."

"Maybe an hour or so, but never for a few days. But don't worry, I'll survive...somehow."

Colin started laughing. "Do you go to boys' school to learn that technique of making leather tops feel guilty about suggesting out of the ordinary ideas?"

"Nope. My abilities come from having an Italian family. And if you ever want to feel guilt, become Italian, become a priest, and then leave to go off and become some man's lover."

The two men parted and Colin made his way back to his office, cursing the fact that it was December and still entirely too warm. Once behind his desk, he called Mary Rose and got her on the first try.

"Hey there, sexy woman," he greeted her after she answered.

"Yeah right Colin. I'm sure that you think that women are sexy."

"Well, Madonna and Cher are."

"Bitch!" she joked over the phone.

"Nice way to talk. Hey, the reason I'm calling is that I'm going to take a long vacation next month. Maybe three weeks, well into February. While I'm doing this, let's neither one of us forget what we were talking about this morning. When I come back, I promise a decision. Is that fair?"

"Perfectly. But listen, I'm about to go into a meeting where some weird nurse is complaining about an equally weird surgeon. I don't mean to cut this short, but..."

"Say no more. I know exactly what you're talking about." Colin hung up the phone, called Daniel and asked if he and Billy were up to the trip. They were. Then he called Dominic and told him of his plans. Dominic was in total agreement and seemed to look forward to the thought of a few days alone with Colin. He agreed to make all the arrangements for everyone, including the few days of hiatus for the various factions within the group.

Chapter 9

Christmas that year was a household, family thing, without the biological families of any of the men involved. Colin's parents were off on a cruise with Derek's again this year, having had enough of the family feast. Al's family made the unusual decision to spend Christmas in Italy with their extended family, and Billy informed his that he would rather stay in town with his new family. Dominic always spent Christmas away from his, preferring the company of whomever he was seeing or in love with at that time of the year. This year, his newfound attraction to Chris was tempered by Chris' decision to go home to Italy for four weeks over the holidays.

Of course, with six homosexuals, Christmas was a culinary delight. The meals for Christmas Eve and Christmas night were spectacular, replete with a perfectly decorated tree and house. The little family had long ago reverted to a smaller number of gifts, each given with some significance attached. Derek, of course, was exhausted from the usual duties associated with running a parish during this time of year. Al welcomed the break from his studies and Colin and Daniel took a little more time off from work. Billy and Dominic didn't seem to make many adjustments, but managed to spend quite a bit of time at home.

On New Year's Eve, it was decided that the group would go out as a group. When someone is involved in leather, going out is a ritual. When there are six leather men involved in going out, the ritual reaches epic proportions. The boys of the group were the quickest to get ready. It was the tops who took a very long time preparing to go out. Dinner that night was prepared by Derek, Al, and Billy; it was a sublime success. It had always been Colin's custom to separate from Derek, and now Al, after dinner as he prepared to get ready to go out. It was a custom that Dominic and Daniel found very attractive, and adopted it as soon as they found out about it. It had already been decided that they would go out in Dominic's new Jeep Commander and that Billy would be the designated driver, not drinking all night. It had also been decided by the tops that there would be a dungeon party for the six of them that night after having a few drinks and some fun at the local bar.

At ten o'clock Dominic, in full leather, made his way over to the other house. Colin was sitting in the library upstairs, sharing a drink with Daniel. "Come on in, and up here," Colin said when he heard the back door. Dominic made his way up to the library on the second floor.

"Ah, I can use a good drink," Dominic said as he prepared himself a gin and tonic.

"It seems like forever since we've had a serious night of drinking," Daniel answered.

"Well boys, lets take it a little slow. We still have three boys that need to be satisfied tonight," Colin added.

"Isn't it our satisfaction that matters most, my dear cousin," Dominic jeered.

"Well, always, of course. But there are times that we must think of others."

"Do they know that we're ready? Where are they anyway?" Daniel asked.

"They are waiting patiently for us upstairs with Billy," Colin said. "They are probably plotting how to get a really hot scene out of us tonight."

"Or having one themselves, as we speak," Dominic kidded.

After they finished their drinks, they called the boys downstairs and made their way out the Dominic's new car. It smelled new. There was just something about that smell that made all men. . . gay, straight, leather, queen. . . melt with satisfaction. They drove the rather short distance to the leather bar that was their usual stomping ground when they went out. Tonight had been advertised as a step back in time; to disco and strict leather dress code. Colin didn't understand why the two were connected. Back then, when the other gay boys were going out for a night of dancing, leather men were crowded in dark, smoky spaces with the backbeat of rock of roll in the background filling in the gaps.

As soon as they walked in, Lee and Michael came bounding

over to say hello and happy holidays. “Hey, neighbors, we don’t see much of you…” Michael said to the group.

“Well now, whose fault is that?” Colin asked.

“It’s probably mine, I’m having a difficult time adjusting to the new place. I miss Philadelphia, and we’ve been there the past week for Christmas. I know, I’ve been a very bad friend. It’s my New Year’s resolution to change that,” Lee said as he put his arm around Colin’s neck and kissed him; a little more passionately than usual than when old friends met, even during the holiday season.

“You’re forgiven. But I’m going to hold you to that resolution. I miss you, and your friendship,” Colin said as he patted Lee on the ass.

While the old friends were reconnecting, in the corner of the bar, well off to the side of the St. Andrew’s cross, three older, darker, and well worn leather men were taking it all in.

“So Joseph, what do you think about that group. If any more of them join up, they will be larger than the Knights,” Dave said, sneering in the general direction of Colin and the family.

“Well, you and I both know that there are way more members than those few men standing over there. But I will grant you, it’s rather impressive. Most leather clubs don’t have as many members as that group,” Joseph answered. John remained silent. He was hoping that tonight wouldn’t turn into one of those vendettas where his two companions were determined to have vengeance for some stupid situation that happened well in the past. He wanted sex; and not with either of them. He was hoping for someone a little younger, like thirty. That would be good; someone exactly thirty years younger than himself. They continued to watch Colin et al have what seemed to be a rather good time at the bar. As a matter of fact, the trio was still standing there watching as what was originally a group of six, left the bar as a group of eight. They would still be staring out into the group of men when the lights came on and they were told to leave the bar as it closed.

Lee and Michael followed Colin and the group back to the house. Lee and Colin seemed to be the only ones a little anxious about having a play party together. Not that they hadn’t had sex, or that they hadn’t watched each other have sex before, but never in the presence of Michael or Derek; or Al, or Billy, or Daniel for that matter. Colin couldn't determine if Lee was still a bottom, and he never knew what Michael was. He assumed he was a top, only because, at one time, Lee was a power bottom.

When they got to the house, the boys started to observe strict leather protocol. They all waited outside while Lee and Michael joined them outside the kitchen door in the back of the house. Once they were inside, Derek, Billy, and Al went downstairs to prepare the dungeon. As the tops, along with Lee, shared a drink in the kitchen, Colin went over to his friend. "Are you OK with this?" he asked.

"I think so. I'm a little self conscious, but I think so. It's just that Michael and I don't do this sort of thing; at least, not until tonight."

"Oh, come on, Lee, you and I have seen each other having sex many times since you've been with Michael."

"But he wasn't there, and neither was Derek," Lee said, looking very nervous.

"But he knows that you do this, right?"

"Well, not exactly. We don't talk about it."

"Lee, now's a nice time to be telling me this. Do you want to leave?"

"No, truth be told, I'm looking forward to it. It has to be done. You and I are friends and I've been avoiding you because of the guilt I carry around, along with that torch that I have for you," Lee confided.

Daniel, Dominic, and Michael finished their drinks and looked over to where Colin and Lee were sharing what seemed to be state secrets. Daniel decided that whatever the intense conversation was about, perhaps a little dungeon time would break the spell. "Are we ready?" he asked, to no one in particular.

Daniel, along with Michael and Lee lead the way down the stairs into the basement. The basement in this house was much nicer than many people's living spaces. The dungeon, well hidden through a series of passages through the immense basement, fooled many an unsuspecting man that these were just more pretend leather people. Dominic and Colin came down last; assuming the position of precedence that everyone in the room, with the possible exception of Michael and Lee, knew about. Once there, he led the other men into the dungeon.

The three boys were already standing in the dungeon,

stripped, except for leather collars and boots. The candles were ablaze and the room was looking oddly comfortable and safe to Colin. He went over to Derek, who immediately fell to his knees. He nuzzled the boy with his crotch before blindfolding him, gagging him, and then leading him to the St. Andrew's cross on the far wall. Once he was sure that Derek was secured against its wood, he went over to Al. For Al, he had chosen a leather hood. Once Al's head was encased in the dark of the leather hood, his arms were attached to chains hanging down in front of the wall opposite Derek. Then, his feet were attached to a spreader bar, so that when he moved one leg, both were affected. Colin looked at Daniel, who took his cue, and, although there was no script, blindfolded Billy and restrained his feet to what looked like a sawhorse with a leather cushion on top. He bent Billy over it and then restrained his arms to the bottom of the opposite side. Billy's ass was in the air, and he was unable to move his arms or his feet. Colin walked over to Michael. He ignored his friend, Lee. "Whatever you feel comfortable with, by all means, do," he said, as he handed Michael a blindfold, "This may help him relax. We're old friends." Michael fixed the blindfold over Lee's eyes.

Colin went to the cross and began flogging Derek. There was very little build up, only rather intense whipping with what appeared to be a very expensive and well-made flogger. As he was doing that, Dominic went over to Al and attached nipple clamps on a chain to the man hanging from the ceiling. After that, he put a parachute ball stretcher around the boy's balls and hung an eight-pound weight from the bottom hook. In an uncharacteristic show of playfulness, he pulled the weight back as far as he could and let it swing freely. Al gasped in ecstasy, which was made visible by the throbbing hard-on sticking out in front of him. While this was going on, Daniel went over and gently put a greased dildo up Billy's ass. It was the type that was inflatable, and, once inside, Daniel used the pump (which resembled a blood pressure pump) to inflate the dildo. He then went around to the other side of the bench and pulled out his cock, letting Billy service him.

Meanwhile, Michael had taken the lead and was restraining Lee to a series of hooks, making his lover face the wall. He picked up a leather paddle and started to paddle Lee's ass. At some point, all the tops in the room seemed to rotate between the boys. Many times, those in the blindfolds and hoods didn't know who was ministering to them, or what was about to happen to them. In the end, it was Michael who finally fucked Al, while Dominic did the same to Billy. Daniel plowed Derek, and Colin finished off by pounding Lee's ass.

Although not planned, and couldn't have been, even with the best choreography and control, the eight men almost all reached orgasm at the same time. The groans and screams of pleasure seemed like some primordial chorus participating in an age-old ritual. When it was over, each Master pulled the blindfold or hood off of their respective partner. Lee was the most surprised of the group.

"Gentlemen, let us take our leave," Colin said, indicating that those in control would go upstairs and clean up. The boys, and this now included Lee were left to the basement to clean up the dungeon and then, themselves.

Once the tops were gone, it was Billy who broke the magical silence, "Man, that was totally fucking hot. Dominic's cock is bigger than Colin's."

Derek and Al started laughing and then looked over at Lee who seemed very anxious. "What's wrong, Lee?" Derek asked.

"That was amazing, but I feel really guilty about being fucked by Colin while you watched."

"Well, I wasn't watching, I think I was busy with Billy's lover at that moment," Derek answered.

"Do you guys do this every night?" Lee asked.

"I only wish. No, these nights are usually reserved for special occasions. It would be great if we did this every night," Al answered.

"No, trust me. You don't want this every night. Then it becomes repetitious and isn't as hot as it can be. We have to use restraint," Derek added.

"Derek's right! We have to save something for special events so we can really get off," Billy added.

For a split second, Derek and Al stood there with their mouths open; they were totally unable to comprehend that it was Billy who just said that. They then burst into laughter, with Billy and Lee joining in. It didn't take them long to clean up the room, put the toys away, and take a communal shower in the basement. Right outside the bathroom was a closet with sweatshirts, socks, and pants for them all to put on. The soon joined the tops upstairs who were similarly attired and draped across each other on Colin's bed, laughing and talking like old friends.

"Why is it that we boys do what we're supposed to do, and have a good time at it, but we always find you tops up here sucking face with each other," Billy asked.

"Because, my child, when there are tops together, even with a boy between them, the passion is between the tops," Dominic said with Colin and Daniel nodding their assent. Michael didn't quite know what to do, he just was happy to be a part of this wonderful group of men.

"It's been a long day for me, I think I'm going home to slip into my bed," Dominic said, sighing.

"You're more than welcome to stay," Colin and Derek said in unison.

"No—after that, I need some space."

"Hold on, we'll go with you as well," Michael said, while Lee looked totally disappointed.

"Hey, the same invitation goes to the two of you," Derek added.

"I know. And I would love to stay, however, I might not ever want to leave. This is so comfortable," Michael answered. Lee seemed to be in a state of shock.

"OK, let me see you guys out. Happy New Year, everyone," Colin said as he saw their friends outside and locked up, patting Finocchio on the head as he went through the kitchen. He looked back at the dog. Finocchio had somehow assumed that the area beneath the kitchen table was his den and he was sitting there looking forlorn. Colin went over to the cupboard and gave Finocchio a treat. Then, and this was done so infrequently, he called the dog and took him upstairs so he could sleep with the rest of the pack, in *their* den.

Chapter 10

Derek was trying to tie up all the loose ends in the parish for his three-week midwinter vacation. He couldn't believe that he was about to go to Washington for MAL, then onto a spa with Al, and then to Amsterdam. He was totally excited, and totally frustrated that he had a bunch of stuff to do, including finding someone to celebrate Sunday liturgies while he was gone. As he was going about his business, he heard the front door to the church offices open and the quiet conversation of a man and a woman. He was hoping against all hope that this wasn't someone coming to tell him that they were getting married.

"Hello," the singsong voice of his bishop rang through the rooms.

"Oh no," Derek said to himself out loud, "not her!"

"In here Millicent," he said as he stood up to greet his bishop and erstwhile friend. When she entered the room, followed by the Rev. Mark Marjoram, his mouth fell open—visibly.

"Well, that's some greeting from a rector for his bishop," Millicent said and she crossed the room and hugged Derek. "You know Rev. Marjoram, don't you Derek?"

"Yes, I do. Please sit down. This is an unusual surprise. I don't usually have my bishop and a well-known evangelical preacher show up on my doorstep unannounced.

"Yes, I apologize for that. But we were in the neighborhood and decided to stop by and tell you of a great new initiative I think that we should begin," Millicent said, turning to Mark Marjoram and patting his hand. Derek raised an eyebrow.

"I've decided that its time that we Episcopalians reach out to our Christian brothers and sisters and start working together in the vineyard of the Lord."

Derek couldn't believe his ears, or his eyes for that matter.

Generally speaking, Episcopalians didn't talk about working in any vineyard, only enjoying a nice vineyard's rewards. And, it was well known that Rev. Marjoram hated homosexuals, was opposed to the basic rights for homosexuals, and advocated a literal interpretation of the Bible. He quietly counted to ten, and then replied, "And this initiative involves?"

"I thought that we could have one of those good old time revival kind of things, with a joint Evangelical and Episcopalian slant. Get the people out, get them excited, get them moving, and coming back to church," Millicent continued.

"At first, I was a little skeptical," Mark Marjoram began, speaking for the first time, "but I see the good bishop's vision and I think that it will do a world of good. Of course, we won't have any of that vestment, holier-than-thou, sort of thing with the restrictive liturgy that you all are used to, but we can certainly come together and forget our differences to announce a new era in Christianity."

"Forgive me Rev. Marjoram, and Bishop, but I'm a little confused. I don't think that the wearing of vestments, or the commonality of the prayer book makes us appear holier than thou. As a matter of fact, I thought that the Book of Common Prayer is our basis of belief. And that being said, surely Bishop, you know that Rev. Marjoram and I stand on opposite ends of the spectrum on many issues. If this is a joint venture, why involve me at all? Just let me quietly disagree and not attend," Derek said, folding his hands and looking directly into the eyes of his Bishop.

As happens so many times when a gay priest is confronted with a particularly disturbing conversation with a non-gay bishop, there was silence; dead silence. Silence so heavy and so dead that it became uncomfortable; and bishops were not used to being made to feel uncomfortable, that was *their* job, to make others feel uncomfortable.

"Well Derek, we wanted to use St. Peter's for the rally point. There are lovely grounds around the church and the local school that borders the back of the property would let us use their facilities and grounds as well. We are...asking permission," the bishop said, folding *her* hands and looking into Derek's eyes with the same intensity that she had received from him.

"As you are well aware, unless we've dispensed with church

law in addition to the Book of Common Prayer, that wouldn't be my decision alone, that would be done with the advice and consent of the vestry. And I can pretty much tell you, they ain't agonna do it."

Rev. Marjoram looked down while Millicent's eyes opened wide. It was a standoff; a standoff that wouldn't have a resolution today. Of course, Millicent didn't get to explain that this was several months in the offing, and that it would not be a fire and brimstone kind of thing. There was so much she couldn't tell Derek. She knew church law as well as he did. After another long silence she said, "Well Derek, would you at least present it to the vestry and let me come and talk to them about it?"

"Of course Millicent. They would love to see you. I'll have the church secretary call your secretary and put it on the calendar. I'll be out of town for the next few weeks, but we can certainly do it in February or March."

As confrontational as the meeting had been, they managed to pull it together and part as civilized WASPs. As they were walking out, Derek shook Mark's hand and asked him about his family life, his church, and other items priests use for small talk. When they got to the door, Millicent turned and hugged Derek, asking him where he would be going for the next few weeks.

"Amsterdam," Derek replied, in a one-word answer that said it all to those in the know. This time, it was the Bishop's eyebrow that went up.

"Well, I hope that it is...er...refreshing, Derek," she said as she took the Rev. Marjoram's arm and walked toward the car. Derek looked on until they were far enough away, and then let out a scream that could only be described as primal. "What in the world is she thinking?" he said to no one in particular. He finished his work, made arrangements, and then made his way back to the house. Al was studying at the kitchen table.

"You are never going to believe what is happening?" Derek said as he went to the refrigerator and grabbed a beer.

"You've decided that the age old WASP convention on not drinking before one in the afternoon is to be discarded?" Al teased.

"My bishop. My bishop is trying to have a revival meeting with Mark Marjoram in my church!" Derek said as he sat down.

"Not that radical guy that I see on television some Sunday

mornings. The one that thinks that we gay men are undermining everything?"

"The one and the same. First of all, I can't believe that she had the unmitigated gall to even bring this up to me. Secondly..." Derek suddenly was at a loss for words.

"Why you?" Al asked.

"Because she needs the space. It's perfect for their little hoot and holler thing. Maybe there are even snakes that they can dance around with. I need to tell Colin."

Al continued to stare out into space, sitting at the kitchen table and then chuckled a bit. He laughed, not because he thought that it was funny, but simply ironic. It also struck him that Derek could sometimes enter a room and leave it, much the same as a hurricane marches across an island. He heard the loud and heated one-sided conversation from the other room as Derek informed Colin of the day's events. Within a few minutes, Derek was speaking calmly again. Colin had that way with Derek. He could calm him down in minutes. He could also rile him up in that same amount of time as well, but today, he calmed the savage beast. Derek came back out to the table and sat down. "Sorry about that," he said to Al.

"That's ok, we all have issues that touch us deeply," Al said.

"Fuck you," Derek said; laughing and getting up, "I'm going to take a shower."

Al continued to sit there, laughing. There was never a dull moment in this household. But it was comforting as well. Finocchio changed positions under the table, looking out from underneath to make sure that no one was surreptitiously eating while he slept. He didn't even get up when Colin's jeep drove into the driveway and Colin came into the house, kissed Al on the top of his head, and said, "How was your day?"

"Quiet, except for Hurricane Derek. Don't push his buttons tonight."

"I wouldn't think of it. Let's go out to dinner. We're going to have to start packing tomorrow and the next day. We are going to be gone for some time, and leather is never an easy accessory to pack."

"Go get Derek and tell him to come along," Colin continued, reaching under the table and patting Finocchio on the head.

"You go get him, I'm scared," Al joked.

Neither one had to go 'get him', he appeared and suggested going out to dinner. Colin and Al smiled at each other, "That's a great idea," Colin said and the men went out to a quiet little restaurant where Derek sometimes railed against his boss and sometimes expressed his excitement about the activities of the next few weeks. Colin and Al didn't say much; they didn't have to. Derek was doing well enough on his own carrying the conversation.

After dinner, they made their way back home and excitedly got out the bags, suitcases, and started the process of determining what they needed to take on the trip, what they wanted to take on the trip, and what they wouldn't be able to take on the trip. As strange as it may seem, it was Colin who was dragging out everything to take with him. A little quirk that was often amusing, and sometimes just downright inconvenient. It would take the three of them two days to finish packing for their trip. Of course, everything that they were taking wasn't going everywhere with them. They were traveling in Dominic's jeep to Washington. Then each of the groups were going their own way, by train, or car, to wherever they were going, and then flying to Amsterdam from Washington. So there was some flexibility with their luggage; but not much.

Chapter 11

It was a crisp January Thursday when the group set out for their extended trip. There were six men in Dominic's Jeep Commander, followed by Lee and Michael in their car, who carried the left over luggage along with them. All the men were dressed alike: black T-shirts, jeans, black boots, and black motorcycle jackets. They looked amusing, all dressed alike, scurrying around their cars as they loaded, unloaded, and reloaded luggage into both vehicles. As they were about to depart, Dominic went into the house to check one last thing. His cell phone rang, "Hello, *caro mio*," Chris' lilting voice came across. "Did you miss me while I was gone?"

"Did I miss you? Of course, I missed you. When did you get back?" Dominic asked.

"Two hours ago, are you busy?" the Italian boy asked.

Dominic then realized that, during Chris' absence he had made these elaborate plans, without telling him. "Well, I'm just about to go out of town for a few weeks, Chris," Dominic began.

"What? When did this come about? Don't you care about me?" Chris replied, almost screaming into the phone.

"I'm going with my cousin and his lovers. We're just spending some quality time together, Chris. Look, it's not like we've been together a long time. I would like to explore that, but, you went to Italy, and I'm going off with Colin for a little while."

"Colin? Colin Morgan, the leather guy? Are you kidding me? He's slime!" Chris said in a staccato voice.

"You know Colin?"

"Yes, when I came to Columbus he lured me. He made me think that he was in love with me and then he told me he had a lover and that he was involved in leather. I think that he wanted me to join in his sick little group and be the new boy toy. I'm sorry, but I just can't imagine showing someone that you love them by beating them. And now I find out that you two not only know each other, but that you're going off somewhere together."

"Chris, we're related. Look, I can't talk about it now. I have to go. I would be more than willing to talk about this when we come back, or to meet you somewhere and discuss it, but I have to go right now."

"Where exactly are you going?"

"First to Washington, then off to Philadelphia and finally to Amsterdam."

Chris hung up the phone. Dominic took a deep breath and then rejoined his friends out in the car. He would talk about this with Colin at a later time, when his emotions weren't so raw. It had finally turned cold in Columbus, and he was happy when everyone was in the car and they started out. The trip was rather uneventful, except for the freaky snowstorm they encountered as they crossed the mountains in Pennsylvania. About five minutes east of Pittsburgh the weather went from gray and cold to almost blizzard like conditions. Once they crossed the mountains and came down the other side, it was simply cold and sunny.

It took several hours, but they arrived in DC Thursday afternoon. Leather men from around the world were starting to gather in the nation's capital, but it wasn't mobbed like it would be tomorrow evening. They checked into the hotel; not the host hotel, but close enough, less than a five-minute walk. Dominic had a suite that adjoined Colin, Derek, and Al's room. That room was across the hall from Billy and Daniel's room that adjoined Lee and Michael's room.

After they all took a nap and then showers, they dressed in casual leather: boots, jeans, jackets, and vests. It was early evening and they walked up to Dupont Circle, stopping for coffee, going to the book stores, and trying to decide among themselves on where to go for dinner. With all of the places they could choose, they went to where all leather men went in January in Washington; a kitschy steak house between Dupont Circle and Thomas Circle. It was warm and cozy inside the restaurant, and that suited them all since the weather outside, while nice, was cold.

"So, what do I have to look forward to?" Al asked the group.

"You've never been here for this?" Lee asked.

"No, Al has led a rather sheltered life," Colin answered.

"Well Al, just remember, you will see more leather men than you can imagine. And you will be tempted, teased, flirted with, and groped. But try to remember your place, with Colin," Dominic said, offering his advice, while he buttered another roll.

"What if I make a mistake?" Al asked.

Colin started laughing. "Al, this is supposed to be fun. It's not a final exam. Try to be aware of your surroundings. Remember your training. Have fun. Two things usually happen here. One, you get caught up in the private parties and orgy yourself into a frenzy. Two, you try to get caught up in the private parties and cruise yourself into a frenzy. We're here to see old friends; to shop at the leather mart; to go to the contest; and spend a little time together, and perhaps, have some fun with a few invited guests."

"I like how you put that," Billy said, sipping his iced tea quietly.

"Well, invited guests are always welcome," Derek added.

"Or we could all have sex together," Lee suggested.

When the waiter came and offered deserts, all the men declined. Chaps and leather jeans can be hot, but not if you have to suck in your belly to button them. They got the check, and then started the brisk walk back to their hotel. As they got closer, Dominic said, "Do you think we could get eight men in one bed?"

"Is that an invitation?" Billy said, and was immediately slapped upside his head by Daniel.

"Look, we've had a big day, the sex will be under whelming, but it might be nice to just curl up like dogs," Dominic answered.

"Speaking of dogs, do you think that Dracul and Finocchio are ok in that kennel? I hope they don't get some disease," Derek said with a worried look on his face.

"It's the best kennel in Ohio, Derek. The dogs will be fine. Let's all go to bed together," Dominic replied.

That night, in what originally seemed to be the biggest king size bed in the world became the most crowded king size bed in the world. It wasn't uncomfortable, and the sex was simple, although all of the men managed to cum. When they finally settled in, they all embraced each other. It looked very much like a posed photograph with arms, legs, and the occasional head peaking out from under the covers.

The next morning all of the men retired to their separate rooms; first for a quick nap, only because the space in their respective beds was so alluring, and then showers. By noon, they were in Dupont Circle again, having lunch and waiting to go to the host hotel to pick up their packages that contained the tickets for the various public events of the weekend.

That night, dressed in their finest leathers, the group of eight men strolled into the lobby of the host hotel and found a vantage point overlooking the crowd. In no time at all, many men came up to Colin and or Dominic and offered their warmest wishes. They had been in the leather community for years, and seemed to know men from all over the world. In many ways, weekends like this were similar to family reunions, with old friends who saw each other only once or twice a year, greeting each other, going over old times and the news of the day.

When the men, mostly the boys of the group, tired of the standing and modeling, they decided to tour the leather mart. This year, the vendors were good, and the quality of the merchandise, excellent. Of course it was way over priced, but it gave the men an opportunity to see, try on, and try out the various clothes and toys that were offered for sale. When they tired of this, Billy was sent back to the rooms with all of their purchases. He was instructed to meet them at the local bar for some serious drinking.

It didn't take long for the men to establish their vantage point again, this time on the second floor of a leather bar. The men in the bar, even those that didn't know them, often nodded in their direction simply because they were such an attractive group. Some of them tried cruising one of the group, or the whole group, with a hope that they would join in the fun later that evening. The eight men seemed to be very much caught up in the joy of their own group. They didn't seem to need anyone else this evening. After a while, they even seemed to tire of the whole thing and went back to their rooms. Even though they all had toys with them, the sex that night was simple; not perfunctory, but simple. Of course, they all played together, and then everyone went to their own rooms and beds. For all of them, it was a fulfilling first day.

On Saturday, the men did pretty much the same thing. At

one point, Al, new to the MAL experience, turned to Derek and said, “Is this all that we do?”

“Yeah, it can be a little boring. I’m not sure why Colin is keeping us so turned in on each other. Usually he’s much more outgoing and we tend to meet new people,” Derek said, stifling a yawn.

“I’m not complaining, its fun and all, and its nice to see all of these guys, but I thought that I would be immersed in the middle of Sodom.”

“That’s just it Al, sometimes its all parties and orgies, and other times, its just run out and buy stuff and get drunk. Colin seems to be watching for something, or someone. And Dominic is like radar, scanning the room as if there is an ominous force somewhere.”

“Boys, what are you two talking about?” Colin asked as he turned to his two lovers.

“Oh, I was just saying that its....” Al began.

“Wonderful!” Derek finished and giving Al a dirty look that he translated as keep quiet, you were about to make a very big mistake.

“Don’t worry, tonight we’re going to a party,” Colin said.

“Who said that we were worried?” Derek asked.

“The look on your face,” Colin said as he turned to get Dominic’s attention. The six of them, minus Lee and Michael who wanted an evening together alone, were going to a party. It turned out that the party was in what appeared to be an abandoned garage. They went upstairs and paid ten dollars each for the privilege of putting their clothing into a large garbage bag, getting a ticket to put in their boot, and then walking around watching men in various stages of sexual pleasure.

In the corner of the garage, three very tired looking older leather men were watching their progress.

“Here they are, again,” Joseph said to Dave.

“Yes, even naked, that Colin seems to think that he commands respect,” Dave answered.

As Colin picked out a man who looked like he came from a Middle Eastern country, they looked in disgust and went off into another and darker corner of the garage. That night, the six men in the group had a great time, and, for once, the boys were satisfied by someone other than members of their leather family. Of course, Colin, Dominic, and Daniel were also satisfied by someone outside the group, but that wasn't as momentous as it was for the boys.

The rest of the weekend was taken up with cocktail parties, brunches, and, of course, the contest. On Sunday night they went to the Eagle. It wasn't crowded at all. Most of the men at MAL had either already gone home or had decided that they had had enough of the nightlife. Or, they had found willing partners to have sex with them.

Monday morning arrived and the eight men were having breakfast in a restaurant/book shop right off of Dupont Circle. They looked tired, and yet, satisfied. It was a good weekend, with just enough sex, drinking, and eating out to make it seem like they had a good time, but not excessive enough to make them jaded and tired.

"So, I can't wait, Dominic, where are we going?" Billy asked with the enthusiasm only a twenty something boy could have.

"Yeah, where *are* we all going?" Derek joined in, looking at Colin.

"Hey, I don't know either. When I said that I would let Dom make all the arrangements, I meant that I would be just a surprised as you guys," Colin answered.

"Well, you know, making four separate arrangements for four groups with entirely different needs wasn't easy. First, let me just start by saying that it is only through Thursday, so if you don't like them, you can certainly put up with it for three or four days. Al and Derek, you're going to take the car to a ski place right outside the district in Maryland. You don't really have to ski, there is an A-frame house that has been filled with wines, food, and enough things to keep you occupied, and get some well-needed rest. Lee and Michael, you're going to a bed and breakfast in Williamsburg, and transportation has been arranged. Billy and Daniel are staying here in DC in a very well equipped condominium right off of Dupont Circle, replete with houseboy." Dominic concluded by looking around the table to see if anyone was really disappointed. No one seemed to be.

"And me?" Colin asked.

"You and I are taking the train to Philadelphia. There's a great old house that I have right off of Rittenhouse Square. It has everything that we need for a couple of days rest."

"And then on Thursday we go to Amsterdam?" Billy asked.

"Yes, the six of you will meet back here and then drive up to Philadelphia. It was easier to get a flight from there. We'll meet Thursday afternoon, get ready, go to the airport and be in Amsterdam on Friday morning," Dominic answered, addressing the group.

"Are you guys sure that this is all OK with all of you?" Dominic asked.

"Yeah – what's not to be OK? We all get to have a couple of days rest before we begin our sleazy Amsterdam trip," Daniel finally added. "Although, I'm not so sure what Amsterdam is like, I've never been there."

"You've never been to Amsterdam?" Michael asked.

"Neither have I," Billy offered.

"Nor have I," Al added.

All eyes were on Colin. Colin had spent a great deal of his youth tramping around Amsterdam. Everyone was waiting for some words of wisdom, to calm or excite the boys that had never been there. Colin appeared reflective and finally, with a very faint smile on his lips said, "Well then, we'll just have to make sure that we show you around."

After breakfast there was a flurry of activity. Colin and Dominic were taking the bulk of the luggage with them since they would be staying in one of Dom's houses, and could easily store the luggage there for the European part of their great adventure. After very quick goodbyes, everyone found their way to the appointed bus, car, train, or cab that they needed and part two of the midwinter break ensued.

Chapter 12

Colin and Dominic arrived at the train station in Philadelphia later that afternoon and were greeted with a huge snowstorm, along with a mysterious attractive Italian boy who came to retrieve them. Dom and the unnamed boy spoke quietly in Italian, which was somewhat amusing because Colin had a marvelous grasp of the language, but he was too tired to pay close enough attention to what was being said. Within a few minutes, they were being maneuvered through the narrow streets of colonial Philadelphia, pulling up to a vintage brownstone that overlooked a small park.

After bringing up the bags, the mysterious Italian boy disappeared, leaving Colin and Dominic alone in the house. Dominic crossed the room and with immense tenderness embraced Colin and kissed his passionately on the mouth. "So cousin, how have you really been?"

"Well, I'm really doing fine Dom. There are moments that are difficult, but basically, I live a charmed life: good paying job, great house, wonderful lovers and built in friends. And a dog."

"Sometimes you look so tired. I was just worried."

"Don't worry about me, but, now that you mention it, I am exhausted."

"Well my prince, we're going to rest. Go up to the next floor. There is a bathroom off of our bedroom. Why don't you take a long, hot bath while I find what there is to eat in the house, and then we can go from there. We can take a nap before we eat, or whatever you want."

Colin, always one to follow suggestions, went upstairs and marveled at the bedroom where their luggage had been deposited. It was huge, with a very large plasma screen television, some overstuffed chairs, a bed that looked bigger than the ocean, and, off to the left, a bathroom that was almost equally enormous. As he undressed, he noticed that there were a lot of bath products; expensive bath products that looked like they had just been placed or replaced there. As he drew his bath he smiled to himself at the picture of this big leather top sitting in a tub full of bubbles with the most marvelous scents that he had ever smelled. When he finally finished, he went out to the bedroom where a sweatshirt and pants were laid out for him.

Al and Derek were equally amazed at the A-frame that they found – found with the help of specific directions, a map, and several answered questions along their route. The cottage couldn't have been better appointed. There were at least eight bottles of wine, enough prepared food from a catering company, a great sound system, and television, movies, CDs, and books. The upper loft had a bed that was simply inviting with numerous quilts and pillows.

"This is quite nice," Al said.

"This is what we both need, I think," Derek added. "I expected Colin to be able to read my mind and pick out what would be good for us, I'm surprised that Dominic had the same ability, unless Colin told him what to do."

"Speaking of doing, what do you supposed they are doing?" Al asked.

"I would imagine that they are fucking."

"Who's fucking who?"

"Whom. And I don't want to know. Lets just get into something comfortable and enjoy this."

"And us, do we get to fuck?" Al asked, with a gleam in his eye.

"Oh yes my lover, you are definitely fucking me tonight," Derek said and the boys went about unpacking and settling in.

Lee and Michael walked into the bed and breakfast in Williamsburg and were amazed. It was simply beautiful and had a huge window that overlooked a colonial scene that was slowly being blanketed by softly falling snow. The ride to Williamsburg had gradually led them to the romantic charm of the colonial enclave.

"I can't believe that we get a few days to ourselves," Michael said.

"Yeah, we need it. Especially after the marathon in DC the past few days," Lee answered.

"Didn't you like it?"

"Of course, what wasn't to like, although I think that you like sex with Colin and his entourage more than I did," Lee said, picking up a suitcase to unpack it.

"I have to admit, it is an attractive thought. To be part of that all the time."

"I don't know, what do we do about our attraction to each other. I wonder how Derek feels about all of this. I mean, he and Colin were together long before Al joined them. And then Billy, who was just a little 'on-the-side-fuck-buddy' seems to have joined them with yet another man. And now Dominic has joined the crowd. Don't they ever get jealous?"

"I don't know. I still don't know how it works, but it sure seems to. Are you having a problem with this? I'm not suggesting that we join the group, but it has been fun, don't you think?" Michael asked his lover.

"Yeah, it has been fun, but..."

"Are you sure that it isn't you that is jealous of Colin and what he has? You've never gotten over him have you?"

"Michael, I'm with you. Colin and I broke up and managed to remain friends. It's just been a little weird the past month, having sex and everything with him again."

"Do you want to blow off the Amsterdam part of this, go back to Columbus and return to our lives?"

"No, I want to go on to Amsterdam. Let's just take it a little slower with Colin. But right now, I want you to fuck me."

Daniel and Billy were marveling at the beauty of the condominium and its multiple floors. As they were walking, arm in arm, up the stairs, the front door opened and the most beautiful blond haired, blue eyed, muscled twenty something young man entered, carrying bags from a very expensive food store. Daniel and Billy just stared for a moment, startled that there was someone in the house, and amazed at how beautiful he was.

"Hi, I'm Eric, the houseboy. You must be Daniel and Billy, and I bet that you're Billy," he said staring into Billy's eyes.

"Yes, we are. I forgot that the house came with a houseboy."

"Well, I'm here. I will take care of anything that you need.

Anything!" he said, going into the kitchen to unpack the groceries.

Billy just giggled at Daniel and the two of them continued up the stairs to their room for a nap. "Well, he's going to be delightful," Daniel said.

"Not nearly as delightful as I'm about to be with you," Billy said, dragging Daniel into the room and literally ripping his clothes off.

Back in Philadelphia, Colin and Dominic had finished a wonderful dinner. At some point, Dominic had managed to freshen up and the two men sat on a couch in one of the rooms. Dominic slid over, and placing his one hand around Colin's neck and his other on Colin's crotch, kissed him tenderly on the mouth. Colin didn't resist, but kissed back and managed to let his hands find Dominic's throbbing hard cock in his sweatpants. Within minutes, they were rolling around on the floor, making out like teenagers. It soon turned into a wrestling match and Dominic easily subdued Colin who was flat on his back with Dominic staring down at him.

"I've wanted you in this position for months now," Dominic said smiling down at his cousin.

"You could have simply asked."

"That wouldn't have been half as fun. Besides, you and I adhere to a code that would never permit either one of us to be seen submitting in front of the boys that serve us."

"Who's submitting?" Colin said, and tried to regain the advantage. He was no match for Dominic who was stronger, a little younger, and a little bigger than Colin. Within minutes, they were naked and Dominic was fingering Colin's hole.

"Are you going to let me do this?" Dominic asked.

"Are you asking?"

Within seconds, Dominic was safely inside Colin, pumping away, while passionately kissing him. Colin's cock was rubbing against Dominic's belly and it didn't take long for Dominic, and then, seconds later, Colin to cum. Even after the last squirt of Colin's cock, they continued to embrace and kiss. It was several minutes before they disengaged.

On a mountaintop in Maryland, Al and Derek were quietly sitting in much smaller, but equally as elegant surroundings, having had a wonderful meal prepared by some restaurant in DC and delivered here before they arrived.

"This is amazing," Al said, not really commenting on what exactly was amazing to him.

"I know. And so are you," Derek said, slipping his hand down Al's pants.

"This is just so weird," he said as he finally stopped talking and started to kiss Derek on the mouth.

"Please play with my nipples," Derek implored.

Al bent down and started nibbling at Derek's nipples. They were almost as hard as his cock. In a scene reminiscent of what had just happened in Philadelphia, the two of them wrestled around on the floor. At one point, Derek demanded that Al spank him; Al gladly complied. When Al finally got Derek into position to fuck him, Derek screamed, "Fuck me hard! Harder!"

It took seconds for them both to climax. When it was over, Al kissed Derek softly on the mouth and finally, after a few minutes, broke the embrace to wash up. He looked over at Derek who was serenely staring at the ceiling.

Lee and Michael made love more passionately than they had with each other for several months.

"Well, I can tell you one thing. Whatever you say about Colin and his troupe, it seems to have inspired you to reach new heights sexually," Michael said, holding Lee in his arms. The scene that had just finished could only be described as being like something a person would see while watching the Discovery channel – two intelligent animals rutting.

"Fuck yeah Michael. I love you," Lee said, nuzzling his lover's chest, and biting at his nipples.

"And I love you Lee."

After Billy and Daniel made love that afternoon, they were quietly asked when they wanted dinner. Daniel made the decision that they would eat about eight o'clock. As he and Billy were walking down the stairs, they heard a small gong sounding. Eric was announcing dinner.

When they walked into the dinning room, it was ablaze with candles and the table looked spectacular. There were fresh cut flowers, decanters of wine, and beautiful china. They sat down as Eric, completely naked, walked in with the first course. Billy giggled.

He was amazed at what older men thought was hot, or what they expected. He didn't find it funny in an offensive way. He just didn't have the imagination or perhaps the experience to orchestrate something like this. Daniel was amazed. By desert, Eric was serving with a massive erection. He was a slight boy – but his cock was easily ten or eleven inches; it stuck out from his slight frame making it even seem bigger. Of course, no one was interested in desert that night. The elegant dinner ended up with Eric's cock up Billy's ass while he, in turn, sucked off Daniel.

On Thursday morning, all six of the gay men gathered in Washington to take the short drive up to Philadelphia in Dominic's Jeep. Lee and Michael would follow in their car. They all appeared refreshed, and definitely relaxed. Once in the car, Billy said, "I hope that Colin and Dominic had as good a time as the two of us did."

"Oh, I'm sure that they did," Derek remarked.

"The thing I can't figure out in that one, is who is fucking whom?" Daniel asked.

"Something I never want to find out," Derek concluded.

They arrived to a Philadelphia blanketed by snow. The meticulous directions that Dominic had given Daniel brought them exactly in front of the brownstone in the old Society Hill section of Philly. They rang the bell and were greeted by an extremely attractive Italian boy who spoke softly in somewhat broken English. As they were maneuvering luggage and people, Derek turned to Al and said, "Well, I can't say that it was exclusive, but I know one cute Italian boy that was probably fucked by both Colin *and* Dominic."

"My thoughts exactly," Al answered.

Colin was sitting in the television room on the second floor when the group arrived. He stood up and was greeted, first by Derek, and then Al, who both said, "I missed you."

And they meant it.

"Not nearly as much as I missed you," and Colin really meant it as well.

There were a few hours before they were to be driven to the airport, and the group spent the time repacking luggage; the task of figuring out what to take and what to leave for the return trip seemed almost monumental, but they managed to make decisions, and come up with manageable luggage for their four day weekend in Amsterdam.

As the arrived at the gate in preparation for boarding the plane that late afternoon, Billy exclaimed, “How will I ever survive, I won’t sleep on the plane and I’ll get there tomorrow. One day will be wasted with me sleeping in order to catch up.”

Dominic laughed along with the rest of the men; “It won’t be a bad thing for you to sleep all day, and go out at night, now, will it?”

“Why don’t I ever think of these things,” Billy sighed.

What none of them had realized when they checked in was that they were all seated in first class, compliments of Dominic. When they called for first class seating, each man looked at their boarding passes to see what seats they were in. Dominic got up first and said, “Well, come on. We don’t get called for first class often.”

Colin turned to Dominic and said, “Thank you so much for this. You don’t know how I hate overseas flights when I’m trying to sleep sitting up.”

“You deserve it, cousin,” was all that Dominic said.

Within two hours of taking off, the men had plenty to drink and eat, and were working out the logistics of the seats that turned into beds. Billy, or any of them for that matter, didn’t have to worry about being able to fall asleep on the plane that night. They all did it easily, and very quickly after getting the seats to recline.

Chapter 13

Friday morning in Amsterdam was cold and gray. Eight very disheveled gay men from America looked perplexed through the whole customs, luggage, getting a cab ordeal. While they *had* slept, they still needed a small nap to be able to experience Amsterdam as it should be experienced. Colin turned to Dominic and asked, "Where are we staying?"

"*The Black Tulip*," he answered with a grin.

"You didn't!" Colin exclaimed.

"You owe me."

"I don't think that I've ever seen a black tulip," Billy conjectured to no one in particular. This brought gales of laughter from most of the men.

"It's a hotel...a leather hotel...with theme rooms," Derek informed his younger companion.

"Who would have thought?" was all that Billy, in his confused state, could say.

"The Dutch," was the answer given by Colin.

Luggage in hand, with customs behind them, the boys got a cab and made the short trip to the hotel. Colin and Dominic had stayed here in the past. For the others, it was the first time that they had been inside the building. Everyone was totally amazed, especially when they went to their rooms. Then there was the men; the men that they past while settling in were, in one word, hot. By the time that everyone was safely checked into the hotel, it was about eleven o'clock in the morning. After a quick poll of the group, it was decided that they first needed a nap – so, they decided to get up at three and start their Dutch experience.

Of course, three meant, wake up at three. By the time that everyone was showered and ready to face the world, it was almost five in the afternoon. As they bundled their jackets against the cold

Dutch winter wind, they stepped out onto the street. Colin suggested a coffee shop first.

"Hey, that's a great idea," Billy said, "coffee will wake me up."

All the men laughed. "What did I say wrong now?" Billy asked.

"Nothing, we will get coffee," Daniel said, smiling.

"Well, duh!" Billy replied.

They did go to a coffee shop and they did, in fact, get coffee. But, as Dominic came back with their mugs of coffee, he had a joint for each one of them.

"Hey, where did you get that? Did you bring it on the plane?" Billy asked.

"No, I just bought it," Dominic replied.

"Aren't you afraid...." Billy continued, but was cut off by Colin. "It's legal here, Billy. And, its sold in the coffee shops, just like this one."

"Hoop-de-da. I'm never leaving this place. First, we're in a hotel with slings and crosses and such, and now I can get stoned right out in public," Billy said gleefully.

That night, the men had a heavy German meal, with a lot of beer. They had done everything wrong to avoid jet lag, and yet, they were still up at two in the morning. Billy continued to marvel at Amsterdam, with each new foray into the dark rooms that most of the bars seemed to have. The sexual tension was high. But, it had been a few days since Derek and Al had been with Colin, so, he let people suck him a little that night, but he fully intended on having sex with the two of them later, and just the two of them. At some point the various couples separated from each other; and Dominic went his own way. Colin, Derek, and Al went back to the hotel and had incredibly poignant sex, made all the more intense because they had a few days separation.

The next morning, eight very hung over gentlemen made plans over breakfast. It would be unheard of for people to come to Amsterdam and not do a museum or two, and that's exactly what they did that morning. After that, it was a quick trip to the leather shop, RoB of Amsterdam. Derek and Al were amazed at the quality of the leather, and were even more amazed as Colin purchased new leathers for all three of them. The quality was excellent, and the price reflected that.

"Should we be spending this much money?" Derek asked.

"Granny's windfall is dong well, we have enough to look good. Not that any of us looked bad, but definitely this is good leather," Colin replied.

Later that night, the boys repeated the previous night's adventures, except this time, they were all eyeing each other, hoping for a little play party back at the hotel. It didn't take long for them to pick up a couple of local guys and suggest just that. Amazingly enough, once back at the hotel, there were so many men, it was hard to tell who exactly was going to do what to whom. There was no real plan, and the scene rambled on for over two hours. When they all finally came, it was amazing. One of the Dutch boys then simply turned to Lee, who was still kneeling on the floor and pissed all over him. Within minutes, almost everyone was pissing on Lee. He seemed to be in total ecstasy. At that point, sex seemed to start all over again, and when someone finally looked outside, it was light out – and in Holland, when its light out in January, it's rather late in the day. None of the men knew what time it was when they finally went to sleep. Sleep and meals had been rather haphazard over the past couple of days.

Late Sunday night, Billy was the first to get up and managed to get everyone else up as well, much like a small child on Christmas morning.

"Hey, Daniel, we can't sleep, its our next to the last night in Amsterdam," he said, nudging his lover out of a sound sleep.

"Isn't it our last night?" Daniel asked.

"Oh no, I hope not," and Billy got up, naked, erect, and ran out of the room, down the hall to Dominic's room. He walked right in and found Dominic asleep, but naked and erect as well. He couldn't resist, he bent down and started to suck Dominic's cock. That woke him up in a hurry.

"Hey, what's up?" he asked the blond buried between his legs.

"We are. But, I have a question. Are we leaving tomorrow or Tuesday morning?"

"Tuesday, Billy."

"Yeah!" and the boy bounded back to his room, leaving Dominic shouting at him about unfinished business.

In a few hours they were all ready again, but this time they went to a nice quiet restaurant for a much-needed meal. There was a roaring fireplace in this place and it kept the winter chill at bay. In many ways, they were all tired. The week before, not to mention all of the drinking, sex, and lack of sleep were beginning to take their toll. But no one was ready to admit that just yet.

"So, is Amsterdam on a Sunday or Monday night like any other gay town on a Sunday or Monday night? Troll night?" Al asked, hoping for an evening at the hotel.

"I don't think so," answered Colin.

"Every night in Amsterdam is so much better than any night in any other gay town, with the exception of San Francisco," Dominic answered.

"So, what do we do tonight that we haven't done yet?" Billy asked.

"We drink, we play, and then, when we are so tired we can't stand up, we play some more," Daniel answered.

"Well, it's nice to see that we've all adopted the Dutch mentality," Lee added.

And that night, they did just that. They drank a lot, and the played a lot; and when the dawn teased the early morning sky, they eventually fell into bed. Monday was spent in much needed rest and relaxation. They shopped a little; this time for souvenirs, and not leather. By evening, the men were ready to have a nice dinner, and, instead of carousing all night long, they were ready for a tender night, each with his respective lover, or, in the case of Colin, his lovers. Dominic chose to spend the evening alone, now feeling guilty for indulging himself while his new found object of attraction was pining away back in Columbus. He had yet to confront Colin about his dalliance with the beautiful Italian boy.

The next morning the boys took up a lot of time packing, and repacking; eight gay men trying to manage to get all of their stuff along with their new purchases into their luggage. By noon they were well on their way home as the plane took off. This time, it was no effort to sleep – they did that very easily and, in what seemed to be no time at all, were landing in Philadelphia.

The dark, unnamed Italian from Philadelphia was there ready to pick them up. Of course, it seemed to take more time to clear customs than it did to fly home. Eight gay men returning from Amsterdam waved red flags in front of the customs agents, and their luggage, as well as their persons, were all thoroughly searched. By evening, they were back in the brownstone in the center of the city. It was finally, at this point, that each man felt the exhaustion from the previous two weeks; no one wanted to cook, or do anything for that matter. They ordered Chinese food, stuffed themselves, and then meandered to the various bedrooms. No one even thought about sex that night. Sleep was their fantasy.

Chapter 14

The cold Philadelphia morning greeted eight very tired men groaning about the long car ride back to Columbus. It was cold and gray, but at least it wasn't snowing, however, no one was excited about the idea of sitting in a car or driving for any length of time. They knew that they had to go back—they had been gone for two weeks, and while they all scheduled some additional time off for recovery, they simply didn't want to begin the process of descending back into the reality of their daily lives.

As they drove away, Daniel asked Al, "So, how does a graduate student get this much time off at the beginning of a new quarter?"

"I'm supposed to be doing some research and writing a paper," Al answered. "But you Michael, how did you get off?"

"Teaching assistants, my dear student, teaching assistants," Michael answered.

"Yeah, I know, I have to be one next term," Al said.

"I just took off work, in case anyone is concerned about how I can get away for a long time," Billy cajoled.

The ride continued on like that through the mountains of Pennsylvania until they crossed into the almost planes like flatness of Ohio. They talked and joked with each other took turns driving and napping, and reading. Lee and Colin were in Michael's car at the beginning of the trip. Somewhere in Ohio, Colin switched with Michael and joined his cousin in the front seat. It was the middle of the afternoon when they finally arrived in Columbus, and home looked wonderful to them. Wonderful, that was, until they drove up closer. On the front of Dominic's house someone had spray-painted: FAG WHORE. And on Colin's was: SICK LEATHER FUCK. Some of the windows were broken in both of their houses. Later they would find that rocks had been thrown through them.

As the men got out of the car, looking shocked at what they found, they stared at their houses and surveyed what had been done to them. Everyone had a different idea of who did what. Billy immediately thought that it was the ominous leather group tracking him down. Derek felt that it was some sort of hate crime. Colin was ponderous. But Dominic knew exactly who it was. "Oh cousin, can I see you a minute?"

"What?" Colin asked.

"Let's go inside," Dominic suggested.

"Don't be so mysterious Dom, what's going on?" Colin said.

"I think I know who might have done this. A nice little Italian boy named Chris," Dominic said.

"Who's Chris?" Derek asked.

"Yeah, who's Chris?" Al asked.

"Was he that hot boy that you took home one night?" Billy asked Dominic.

"Do you see everything Billy?" Dominic asked.

"You know Chris?" Colin asked.

"Who is Chris?" Derek asked again.

"A graduate student from Italy that I fucked, and apparently that Dominic fucked as well. But that doesn't explain what has happened here. I mean, the guy didn't really like me much, but what did he have against you, Dom?" Colin explained.

"You. He got all mad because I was going away with you," Dominic answered.

"Who the fuck is this Chris?" Derek asked, hands on hips and staring coldly into Colin's eyes.

"Like I said before, he is a graduate student. I met him on a plane, and, when you were being all pissy, I fucked him one night, end of story," Colin said.

"Does this happen often?" Derek asked.

Colin was indeed perplexed. He couldn't figure out why Derek was making an issue of this. Of course, broken windows and spray paint on the house could have something to do with it. They all went inside. Nothing else seemed to be disturbed, so they called the police. Of course, the alarm agency had already done that and the police had simply written it off as vandalism. Since nothing was terribly disturbed, other than broken windows in January and a spray painted house, the men decided that they were fairly lucky. When they were all settled in, and the window repair people were called, everyone calmed down a notch or two. The repairmen would be there that afternoon and the problem of cold wind blowing through the house would be taken care of. Al and Derek cleaned up the broken glass and the rocks.

"Sir, I'm sorry about that outburst out there," Derek said, pulling Colin aside.

"You don't have to apologize, you have every right to be upset about something like this," Colin answered, putting his arm around Derek.

"It's just usually, I know what's going on. I guess I really was in my own world when this happened."

"No problem. I felt guilty about it because you were so distant, and that made the whole thing even more of an intrusion."

Dominic walked in on their conversation. "Sorry, did I intrude?"

"No, not at all," Colin answered, "but why are you so sure that this was Chris?"

"Something about the intensity of his reaction when I was going away with you. I mean, he and I had sex a few times before we left, but there was nothing about a long-term commitment or anything like that. As a matter of fact, he had been in Italy for almost a month prior to that. I mean, I could be wrong, but I don't think so. However, we can certainly find out."

"How? Ask him?" Colin asked.

"No, after that time of unpleasantness with Billy, I installed a camera between the two houses. It's activated by motion and we simply have to watch the tapes," Dominic answered.

After the workmen arrived, Colin and Dominic went over to Dominic's house to review the tapes. Dominic's hypothesis about Chris was correct. He was caught on tape, in the act of spraying Colin's house. He didn't even try to hide his identity other than having a hooded sweatshirt under his coat. What was frightening about the tape wasn't just that here was a man openly vandalizing their homes, it was the maniacal look on his face as he did it.

"What do you think about that?" Dominic asked.

"I think that we might have a real bunny burning crazy on our hands," Colin answered. "What do you think we should do?"

"Well, I think that I have to pay Mr. Chris a visit."

Colin walked back home. By the time that he arrived, the windows were finished, and some cleaning group was removing the spray paint. Surprisingly enough, it came off very easily. While they were working, the window repair people were working on Dominic's windows.

Meanwhile, in a bar across town, three weary older leather men were sharing cocktails during happy hour. They didn't fit in with the collegiate crowd, but that didn't seem to bother them. It also didn't bother them that they had reached the invisible stage for twenty something men. Invisible, not so much because of their age, but invisible because of their age and the apparent lack of care they took in their appearance.

"Where do you think the little leather family is?" Joseph asked.

"I don't know – they haven't shown their faces in town since they left. They must have gone somewhere, but there appears to be eight of them now. Where would a hoard like that go?" Dave continued.

"Maybe some leather party that we don't know about," John added.

"Remember, there's nothing that *we* don't know about," Dave said.

"Well, wait until they get back. Who do you think did that to their house?" Joseph asked.

"Oh probably some antigay thugs trying to scare them because they are so open about what they are doing. You would think that they have resurrected the Mormon practice of polygamy," Dave answered.

"I still think that they need taught a lesson, they are destroying our leather club. And we do have our rules," Joseph said to the other two men.

"Don't you think that we've done enough to them? I mean, most of our brothers don't agree with our view of leather. I'm not so sure that I agree with it. It was unfortunate what Brandy did, but it's over now. As for the Arab boyfriend of the mobster? That was another unfortunate accident, but it affected them. We can't be involved in murder, no matter how unintentional it may be," John said to Joseph.

"Well, we need to scare them, at least," Joseph added. "We can't have them thinking that they got one over on us. Let's have a dungeon party out in the woods again, and really teach them a lesson."

"Do you really think that they would come? They aren't stupid," Dave cut in. "But we need a good old fashioned dungeon party."

"We have to be careful. The police are kind of looking for us, although they can't believe that there is an international club that is involved in kinky gay sex," Joseph cautioned.

"And, remember, the European guys, the ones that are really in charge of this group, aren't particularly happy with us. And remember also, that Dominic and Colin both have ties to a former leader of that group," Dave added.

"That was ancient history, Dave," Joseph said.

"We could try to get them to that initiation coming up in the South," John suggested.

"No, there's that weird Mark guy coming in then. He's a problem. First, he's somewhat of a public figure, so he wants the whole thing conducted with an executioner's mask on, and I don't think that it's going to work," Joseph added.

"What kind of public figure is he? Famous?" John asked.

"None of us know. He just appeared at one of our play parties and started beating this guy. He was a true sadist. And let me tell you, he brutally fucked the guy," Dave answered. "I don't know who he knows, but he's one cruel person."

"You're ones to talk. I mean, what about that doctor in Pittsburgh and the Arab boy in West Virginia? Why did that happen?" John challenged.

"You're out of line John. Those were basically accidents. Well, the first was a problem because no one knew that Brandy was a total mess. The second one was simply because someone went too far in trying to avenge what happened in Pittsburgh," Dave said, motioning the waiter to bring another round over.

"Dave, this has to stop. We can't continue this vendetta. Basically Colin is a shit head when it comes to leather. Nothing is good enough for him. But that doesn't mean that we have to stalk all of the people around him."

"John, we're not. But a couple of us have gotten into trouble, we just want to be left alone to do what we do best, rough play. He can't get involved in it."

"I don't think that he is. I just think that he's protecting his family, Dave."

"Boys, boys. Stop this bickering. I'm not sure what the answer is. I know that we can't contact anyone in the Order because they wouldn't approve of what has happened. So far, the name of the club hasn't appeared anywhere, and no one is challenging us to explain what has happened. But I do know that if Colin did have the information, he would definitely use it against us, and we have to avoid that," Joseph said, weighing in on the matter.

"So, where's this play party and when?" Dave asked.

"I'm not sure where it is, or the date for that matter. I do know that we'll be told soon enough. But Dave, you and John are definitely coming."

The men spent the rest of the evening eyeing the customers and wait staff of the bar. At one point, Chris entered the bar and walked past their table. Joseph reached out to grab hold of his arm. Chris, looking startled, simply said, "Drop dead, looser," and kept on going through the bar. Dave and John simply looked at each other with raised eyebrows, but didn't say anything.

Back at their houses, Colin, Derek, Al, Billy, Daniel, and Dominic were going over the events of the past few weeks, explaining about who Chris was and why he would do something like this. Dominic concluded that he was probably very highly strung and maybe even suffered from some psychological disorder.

"He might be a borderline personality. Or, he just might be a major drama queen," Al suggested.

"Well, he's weird, that's for sure. Do you think that we're safe?" Billy asked.

"I'm going to visit him and reason with him. Of course, he simply could have been very angry and just wanted to lash out at us," Dominic answered.

"I just didn't think that he was like this. He was so charming when I first met him," Colin said, genuinely sorry for bringing yet more stress into their lives. “I apologize guys, I didn’t think that it would end up like this.”

“Well, at least he didn’t end up joining the family and living here. Good thing we found this out before that happened,” Billy concluded.

All of the men started laughing. However, Colin didn’t laugh all that long. As he sat there contemplating his life and his family, he started to wonder: who is a part of this family? Of course Al and Derek formed his immediate family, but had the past few weeks started to include Billy, Daniel, and Dominic? Had they progressed from a three-way marriage into a six-way marriage with two clearly delineated levels in the family? Colin didn’t know how he felt about all of this. He truly loved each one of these men, but Derek and Al were definitely much closer to him than Billy and Daniel. And Dominic…he was family in a different way.

“Has anyone checked with Lee and Michael? Was their house OK?” Daniel asked.

“Yeah. I called them. They are fine. Well, they’re exhausted, and I’m not sure if anything that I said sunk in, but they seemed glad to be home and, I think that they wanted to be alone and not be involved in anything else,” Derek said.

That night everyone went to bed early. The trip, the anxiety, the shear exhaustion had taken its toll. It didn’t take any of them long to fall asleep. Earlier in the day, Billy had gone to the kennel to retrieve the dogs. Dracul and Finoccchio were happily in each of their houses, with their respective master/pack. Somehow, the men felt safer with a dog in the house. Not that the dog could adequately defend them, but they sure could warn them of any danger.

Chapter 15

The next morning, Derek, Al, and Colin decided that they would stop by their respective offices and check email, messages, and make sure that their enterprises had not suffered from their absence. They weren't going back to work for real until Monday, except for Derek who, of course, would start on Sunday. But Derek was the first one out of the house that morning, over to the church offices. He had several voice mail messages and email messages from his bishop. He decided to test the waters by calling her office before nine.

"Bishop Barclay," Millicent answered.

"Wow! I expected voice mail. Hi Millicent, this is Derek."

"Back from the den of iniquity?" the bishop asked.

"Yes, back from everything, and about to delve into some of this business, even though I'm not officially back until Sunday."

"Well, I hope that you're rested."

"You know what happens when you go on vacation...you need a vacation to recuperate from the vacation, especially when a transatlantic flight is involved."

"Derek, it has been so long since I've gone on vacation, I simply don't remember. But, I'm glad that you're taking care of business. So, what about the faith rally at St. Peter's?" she asked.

"Is that what you're calling it now? That is just so un-Episcopalian, Millicent."

"Derek, do you always have to challenge me? There was a time when we were close. I miss that time. Being a bishop isn't easy, there are so few people I can trust and open up to."

"Millicent, you can always trust me. I'm fairly non-judgmental, unlike the Rev. Marjoram that you are hanging out with these days."

"He does have his issues, I'll grant you that, but don't you think he's attractive?"

"Well, there's a non-sequitur for you. Attractive? I'm not sure about that one – the man hates me, and my kind, for that matter. But what do you care?"

"He's unmarried Derek – well, widowed, his first wife died."

"Of embarrassment?"

"That certainly wasn't Christian of you, Derek. But, we've been getting rather close."

"Millicent, be careful. You're a bishop – a divorced bishop, and he represents a brand of Christianity that doesn't exactly fit in with our beliefs. The Church is certainly changing its attitudes, but this might be too much of a step for it to take."

"Well, it's in its infancy yet. So, tell me, did the vestry OK our plans?"

"I really haven't check with them yet, but I have to tell you, I seriously doubt it."

"Well, you know Derek, I can overrule them, or, for that matter, so could you."

"Do you really think that would be prudent, Millicent?"

"Well, let's cross that bridge when we come to it. Look, I have to run, let's do lunch sometime soon. I miss our friendship."

"So do I, Millicent, take care."

While Derek was discussing life and liturgy with his bishop, Colin had managed to arrive at his office and was madly going through a very long list of emails. There weren't many voice messages; Martin had taken care of that for him. There was one from a potential client, one from Mary Rose, and a couple from company representatives that wanted to wine and dine him with the expectation that he would suggest the use of their materials.

He decided to call Mary Rose and get it over with.

"Good morning, this is Mary Rose," she answered.

"How can you always be so cheerful?" he asked.

"Where have you been? Where did you go?"

"Many places, but I just got back from Amsterdam."

"I am so jealous. I can't believe it. I've not been to Europe in a while. But, I'm about to run off to a meeting – did you think about the offer?"

"Yes I have, and I'm going to bring it up to my family

tonight."

"How many are there in that family at the moment?"

"I'm not so sure myself. But go to your meeting. I'll officially be back in the office on Monday; I'll give you a call them."

"Good-bye my love," and Mary Rose hung up the phone and went off to her meeting; the heels of her shoes clicking all the way down the hospital corridor.

Colin finished up quickly and returned home. Well, he returned to Dominic's house, only to find Dominic ready to go out the door.

"I'm glad you're here, I was just about to pay Chris a visit. Do you want to go with me?" Dominic asked.

"Do you think that it would be prudent?"

"I could use the moral support."

"Dom, since when do you need moral support?" Colin asked.

"I'm not sure about this guy – he might be crazy and it would be nice to have someone there."

"Sure, I'll go – my car is warm, let's use it," Colin suggested.

The two men made the short trip to Chris' apartment. When they rang the bell, he answered the door by simply staring at them, speechless.

"So, it's the leather mafia on my ass again. What do you two want, to beat me up or stick your feet up my ass?" he sneered.

"Chris, I need to talk to you," Dominic said, crossing the threshold and holding out his hand to pull Colin inside as well.

"You two lay a hand on me and I'm calling the police."

"Go right ahead Chris," Dominic said, "and we can tell them about your little act of vandalism."

"Why do you think that it was me that did it?"

"The surveillance tapes clearly show you doing it, Chris. We don't want to call the police, and we don't want to make you pay for it, and we don't want to hurt you. We want you to promise never to do that again," Dominic said very quietly.

At that point, something happened that neither Dominic nor Colin could have predicted. Chris began to cry. He wasn't simply crying, he was actually sobbing. Through the sobs they could hear him saying that he only wanted to be loved. It was Dominic who went over to the young Italian man and put his arm around him. Chris didn't seem to respond, he only kept on sobbing. After a few minutes, Dominic stepped back and said, "Look, let's let bygones be bygones. No permanent harm done. You're a beautiful man, Chris. Perhaps we just met at the wrong time."

Chris didn't respond, and, after a few minutes, Dominic gave Colin the sign that it was time to leave, which they did. When they got outside, it was Colin who spoke first. "Well, that was really weird. I think that you might be right. That boy has some serious psychological or emotional problems."

"I thought so, simply from his reaction when I was off on a trip and wouldn't cancel it to be with him," Dominic replied.

"I just feel like we should be doing something for him. He seems so pitiful in there."

"Pitiful at the moment, but we've seen what he does in addition to the crying act."

"True."

When the two of them returned to their own neighborhood and got out of the car, Colin asked, "Do you want to come over? I might be all alone at the moment, and I could use the company."

"I'm sorry Colin. I think that I might need some time to myself."

"I understand."

Colin went to his house, opened the door and looked for a place to collapse. He wasn't finding that place readily, so he went into the kitchen, and, without looking under the table, said hello to Finocchio. He could hear the thump, thump of the dog's tail. He grabbed a snack and something to drink and made his way up to the library on the second floor.

He seemed to melt into the large, comfortable chair with the matching ottoman. He picked up the novel he had started before his trip and opened it. That's how Billy found him when the younger man came home. Without saying a word, Billy went over, squeezed into the chair with Colin and curled up beside him. Within minutes, the two of them were sound asleep.

Hours later that was exactly how Derek, and Al found them, asleep in the chair, curled around each other. Standing in the doorway with their arms around each other, the three of them smiled at the picture they saw before them. Finally, Derek said, "I think that I should probably be jealous, or something."

"Or something," Al answered. "But who could be jealous of the two of them. They just are so... like together. Not in the same way Billy is with Daniel, or you and I are with Colin, but kind of joined somehow . . . maybe spiritually. Which one of us is cooking dinner tonight?"

"Let's do it together," Derek answered. The two men quietly went downstairs and started to search around for something to prepare for dinner. By the time that Daniel came home, dinner was almost ready. As he bent down to pet Finocchio, he looked up at Derek and Al and said, "How was your day? Is Billy at the bookstore, today?"

"Billy is curled up in Colin's arms upstairs," Derek deadpanned.

"Derek, don't be so..." Al started, but Daniel stopped him, "That's OK. I know that they are close, and I know that Billy loves me."

"That's nice," Billy said looking into the room from the back stairs. Colin was right behind him with his arm on Billy's shoulder.

"Look, my Lord, the servants from below stairs are talking about us again," Colin said.

"Yes, Your Royal Highness, should I have them beaten?" Billy continued along with the joke.

"No...they would like that entirely too much. What's for dinner?"

"We made pasta fagioli," Al said.

"What's that?" Billy asked.

"Rigatoni with beans...." Daniel answered.

"Well, I guess there's no sex tonight – at least not the kind I was looking for," Billy said as he stepped down into the kitchen. Derek threw a kitchen towel at his head and the men gathered around the kitchen table for dinner that night. As Daniel and Billy were cleaning up, Colin decided to tell Derek and Al about the job offer.

"Hey, Mary Rose has a job for me back in Pittsburgh," Colin said without any emotion, testing the waters, mostly of Derek and Al.

"I thought the whole purpose of you having your own company was having the freedom to come and go as you please," Derek responded.

"True, but, the salary on this one is kind of amazing. She's up to $250,000 per year with some nice perks."

"Do the perks include an organized gay community in Pittsburgh?" Derek challenged.

"Hey, I'm not saying I would take it, I'm just passing along some pertinent information."

"That is a lot of money," Al added.

"This is kind of preliminary, and I don't have really strong feelings about it one way or the other," Colin said, taking Derek's hand in his.

"Hey, Pittsburgh is a long way to go for a hot time," Billy said. Daniel was keeping quiet, but was distressed by the news. He didn't want to loose the close friendship that he had with Colin, not to mention the hot sex, and he didn't want to test the waters of where Billy's true loyalty rested.

"Well, the two of you would be welcome wherever the three of us are," Colin said.

"Yes Billy, you and Daniel have become a part of us," Derek added, turning around to smile.

Everyone in the room fell silent for a minute. They were shocked that Derek was being so totally kind to Billy. At one point Al looked at his lover and started to smile. Then everyone started laughing. "Hey, what is everyone laughing about?" Derek asked.

"Well, we're just kind of shocked that you're being nice to Billy," Colin said.

"Who said I was being nice to him, I was being nice to Daniel. Billy is just with him," Derek joked.

They all started to laugh, but Daniel was glad that they considered him important enough to be involved with discussions about where they would live and work. The men did discuss it for a while, and it became apparent that no one was really interested in going back, but the thought of significant income would be something that they, including Billy and Daniel, would think about during the next few days.

"I have some time before I have to give Mary Rose and

answer, and, if we miss this chance, no big deal, the company is doing well," Colin said as the men retired to the living room with a couple of bottles of wine. No one had to go to work for the next couple of days, and it just seemed right to build a fire, sit around with some wine, and talk for a while.

"Well, it has been a momentous few weeks, even the arrival back home was filled with drama and intrigue," Daniel said.

"I can do without anymore of that kind of drama in my life," Derek said as he curled up in Colin's arms.

"I'm sorry about that guys. I never thought that what happened a few months ago would have such an impact. And I really never thought that he was that off."

"So, is Dominic going to continue to fuck him?" Billy asked.

Laughing, Colin answered, "Well that was direct, but I don't think so. There is that whole Italian thing going on. I doubt that Dominic would want to couple with him again after having his home and security violated like that."

"So, when's our next trip to Amsterdam?" Billy asked.

All of the men in the room were laughing out loud at that one. They hadn't recovered from the trip to MAL, or the European trip, or the return home, for that matter. "Well Billy, lets see about getting back into a routine, and getting some rest before we decide to go off like that again," Colin answered.

"I did like the feeling of freedom, at least, sexual freedom, that I experienced there," Al added. "It would be wonderful to live somewhere without the bias that people in this country seem to have about us."

"Sometimes, even gay men have a problem when I start talking about leather," Billy added, "And I'm cute. Who do they think they are?"

"Well, that's one way of looking at it," Derek said and all the men started laughing. Not only was Billy's comment amusing to them, but, at that point, they had drank a lot of the wine.

On the other side of town, in an empty warehouse, Joseph and his two sidekicks were having a little party. They had several bottom boys tied up and had just finished flogging them. John didn't understand where they got these cute younger men, and why they never seemed to have any real sexual connection with *them*, only each other, but he went along with it because they were his friends and knowing he was well past the cruising age and that he no longer had the ability to pick up young men in bars. Tonight, the scene with them ended quickly, almost before it had begun. The four or five boys, he couldn't remember, literally ran out of the warehouse, after the three of them had brought each other off.

"That was fulfilling," Joseph said.

"How come we never fuck them? Or blow them? Or do something to them that involves our cocks or their cocks?" John asked.

"We don't need that – they get us hard, and that's all we need from them," Dave answered for Joseph.

John thought to himself for a minute, 'well, yes, that's all you need, I could use a little more', but he didn't say anything. The three of them went over to the corner and picked up the bags that they brought with them. Dave pulled out a bottle of gin and then some tonic and a baggy full of lime slices. John couldn't believe that they had packed a picnic lunch for an orgy. Of course, since the sex was always between the three of them, it probably didn't matter much. He wondered why he never seemed to see these boys that they played with outside of the dungeon parties or orgies.

"So, when is that new initiation in the South?" Dave asked.

"Next week, actually. On the 15th – it should be warm down there, but not too warm," Joseph answered.

"How many are being initiated?"

"Only the one, this Mark guy."

"I'm not so sure we should be letting him in. He really doesn't seem to like gay people, and I think he's just infiltrating," John said.

"Well, I think we have to rely on the fact that he's been checked out, and that he's been nominated by a trusted member, and seconded by another," Joseph said.

"Is that Daniel guy being invited?" Dave asked.

"Well, there's an idea. We should do it, simply to make him nervous. I doubt that he would go," Joseph answered.

"It would be fun to watch him squirm. Maybe make his boyfriend nervous as well, but he might just inform the police of what we're doing."

"We could do it another way. Tell him the date and the

location, but have someone meet him at the location we give him, and then take him to the real location. That way, if it is a setup, we're covered."

"That's a great idea, Joseph. Why didn't I think of that? Too bad we can't get that Colin Morgan down there, or one of his boys. I would love to beat the hell out of one of them."

"We could do that, but there would be severe repercussions. Remember, Heinrich was his mentor, actually his Master for a while. He's protected, on many fronts. We would probably be drummed out of the club."

"Well, if he's protected, why do we continue to harass him and his family?" John asked.

"I don't like him. Period. And, in addition, it's because of him and that twink that Brandy is in jail, and, for that matter, our other friend as well," Joseph answered.

"Too bad we can't do something," Dave said.

"Well, maybe we can, I'll have to think about it. But we will have to be careful, whatever we decide," Joseph answered.

"I think we should just leave him and his alone," John replied.

"What you think doesn't matter," Joseph said.

The three of them sat there drinking their gin until they were almost drunk, and then they staggered out of the warehouse and got in their car. John drove very slowly because he wasn't quite sober; not drunk, but definitely not sober either. He left the other men off and drove on home. When he got to his house, he went into his bedroom, drew the curtains, laid down on the bed. He reached into the top drawer in the table beside the bed. He didn't even think about what he was doing—he pulled out the gun, opened his mouth and shot himself.

Chapter 16

Billy was cleaning the house on Monday morning after everyone had gone off to work. He still hated Mondays, primarily because he had to clean, and because he was alone. He preferred it when the house was full of people and activity. This morning, it was just him and Finocchio, who followed him around while the boy did his chores. After he was done cleaning, he was supposed to go to the store and do the grocery shopping for the house, and then do some of the laundry. He wondered if this is what his mother had done her whole life, and he thought to himself, 'boy, if that's the totality of your existence, it's pretty bleak'.

As he was about to take a short nap between cleaning and the shopping, the phone rang in their apartment on the third floor. "Hello," he answered.

"Daniel, please," the voice said.

"He's at work. Can I take a message?" Billy asked.

"OK, tell him the 15th – be at the train station in Filbert, Georgia. Get a car, go down route 5 for 10 miles, turn left at the old Sunoco station, and open the gate, go until he sees all of us."

"What? Wait a minute, who are you? I have to find something to write this down."

"Were you born stupid or did that happen later in life?" the voice said.

Billy found a pen and the nameless voice repeated the instructions. When he hung up the phone, he felt very nervous. It didn't take a genius to know who these people were. He was literally paralyzed with fear. He thought that once Brandy was put in jail back in Pittsburgh, this would all be over. Boy had he been wrong. He called Daniel first.

"What did they say?"

Billy recounted the whole story, including the comment about him being stupid. When he was finished, he said, "Daniel, I'm scared. Are they coming after me?"

"I don't think so, but I'll finish up here and be home quickly. See if Dominic is home, and, if he isn't, get his dog over there with you."

After he hung up with Billy, Daniel called Colin who said that he would go right home. He suggested Dominic, but of course Daniel had already done that. Within the next hour Colin, Daniel, and, by chance, Derek arrived home to find Dominic and Billy sitting in the living room of their house. Al still was in the dark about what was happening, but he was having tests today at school anyway.

"Hey Billy, don't worry, I honestly don't think that we have anything to worry about," Colin said.

"I know, it's just that it brings back a lot of memories; memories that I really don't want to remember right now."

By the time that Al arrived home, he was slightly amused to find all of the men in the living room; amused, that is, until he saw the looks on their faces. "Did somebody die?" he asked.

Everyone laughed at the Italian stereotype. "Boy, you *are* an Italian. No, no one has died. The Dark Knights of whatever have contacted Daniel about coming to a meeting next week," Derek answered.

"Well, I think that we should call the police and let them know that the group that managed to kill Vlad and Amin are meeting again," Colin said.

"I'm not so sure that we should do that. After all, maybe they aren't all bad. By alerting the police, aren't we just setting up for another raid on a gay sex party?" Dominic asked.

"I don't think so. This group is rather ominous. Maybe they need to be raided. It's not that I don't see your point, I do. It's just that I want them to leave us alone, and, if they are engaged in activity that would jeopardize the welfare of young gay men, bottoms or tops, I want it to stop."

"I just don't know about the police. They can be so police-like at times," Dominic said.

"Well, what about my friend, the assistant district attorney in Pittsburgh?" Colin asked. "You know him Dominic."

"Patrick is a good guy, we all went to school together. I do trust him, why don't you give him a call."

"You know the DA in Pittsburgh?" Billy asked.

"Yes, we know each other," Colin answered.

"Why didn't you contact him with the whole Brandy affair?"

"I did, why do you think that it went so smoothly for you."

No one felt like cooking that night, so they ordered out for Chinese – an immense amount of Chinese food. After they ate, Colin went into the library and called his old friend, Patrick Monaghan, the assistant district attorney in Pittsburgh. His wife answered, and, after attempting to screen the call, passed it along to Patrick.

"Patrick, this is Colin."

"Hello there, long time no talk."

" I know Patrick, I just didn't think that you needed to talk to someone involved in the biggest scandal in Pittsburgh."

"Not to mention, Columbus. How is your cousin? Has he gotten over Amin's death?"

"Sometimes I think that he has, and other times, I think that he never will; but that's kind of why I'm calling. The group that the two guys belonged to that committed those murders has tried to get in touch with one of my friends. Apparently there is a meeting coming up next week. I thought that maybe you might want to get in touch with law enforcement and get to the bottom of what has been going on."

"Where's the meeting?"

"Somewhere in Georgia."

"I certainly don't have jurisdiction there, but I could contact the local authorities."

"Could you do it with some sensitivity? I don't want this to be a gay witch-hunt. I just want these guys caught and stopped, especially the ones that keep bothering our group."

"Group? How many people are you in bed with Colin?"

"Does it matter to you?"

"No, just curious, but I can tell you...if every straight man realized how much sex, not to mention the variety of sex that you gay guys have, there wouldn't be a heterosexual marriage for years to come."

"Well, essentially just the two lovers. However, Billy now has a lover and they live on our third floor."

"I always thought that you were porking Billy."

"I do from time to time, but he's not a lover, or a regular. But, haven't we gotten off the track?"

"Yes we have. I'll have someone get in touch with you about all of this. Give me the date and what you know."

Colin did just that. At the end of the conversation, he had one last question. "Patrick, none of this will involve Dominic, will it?"

"No Colin, we can keep him out of it."

After that the two men hung up. Colin went back down to the living room and told the group about his conversation. Billy and Daniel seemed somewhat relieved. As the men sat around discussing the issue over and over again, Derek decided to change the subject.

"You will never guess what..."

"What?" Daniel asked.

"Millicent, bishop of the Episcopal church, has fallen for the weirdo Mark Marjoram and wants to pursue a relationship with him."

"I've never approved of mixed religion marriages," Colin said.

"That guy is just strange," Daniel added.

"Yeah, there's something off about him," Dominic joined in. "I've always thought that he might be gay."

"He was married, to a woman once," Colin said.

"What happened to her?"

"She died."

"Of boredom or embarrassment?" Daniel asked.

"Are divorced bishops permitted to remarry?" Al asked.

"Well, I think that they are, but they need the permission of the standing committee, or at least, as a courtesy, they need to tell them about it. And you're right; the whole religion thing is bound to come up. I actually met him. He wasn't friendly. He was kind of attractive in that wholesome self-righteous way, but he creeps me out."

"Millicent has always been a sort of lost child, never quite fitting in. Her first marriage was a total mess, but that wasn't her fault. Her husband was a real piece of work," Colin said.

"Yeah, he was. She really is a needy woman and maybe

that's why she manages to have substandard relationships. She falls into them too quickly," Derek continued. "But I don't even know if there is a relationship, or if she's just fantasizing about it, or, maybe a better way to put it would be that she's planning it."

"The trials of heterosexuals elude me," Billy said.

"Well, this was a great first day back at work," Daniel said.

All of the men laughed uneasily. Dominic and Colin got up to walk the dogs. At first, everyone wanted to go with them, but then, they decided that they would feel more comfortable at home. It had been a while since Dominic and Colin had been alone, not since the few days prior to going to Amsterdam.

"Nice cold night we have here," Colin said.

"Yes, it is. The dogs like it."

"How do you know?"

"I'm guessing. I don't think that Chris will bother us any more, but I didn't know that you had slept with him."

"Dom...you can't mean that there was something in my life that you didn't know about, do you?"

"I guess I'm slipping."

"Does it bother you that I slept with him? I found him first, remember."

"No, not at all. I don't know. This whole thing with this leather group has me in a very bad mood. It's bringing all those memories of Amin back. I really haven't managed to get over him."

"Cousin, maybe you never will. Maybe there will always be an empty spot in your heart. After all, he was ripped from you, with no time to prepare. Perhaps you will just have to go on, and somehow manage to keep your head above water."

"Interesting. You are the first person to say that I might have to go on and try to salvage a life. Most people tell me that, with time, I will forget."

"I don't think that you will ever forget. I know that I won't. Sometimes I think we advise people to put things in the back of their memories and go on. I think that we just have to accept that something very horrible has happened to us. Whatever happens in the future will not change that. There may be better times ahead, a more promising relationship, a more incredible sexual experience, but that doesn't mitigate the pain that we feel from a loss so horrible and unexpected."

"You're kind of philosophical tonight, Colin"

"I know. This whole thing has me crazy as well."

"I want to go along with whomever Patrick sends to investigate."

"Dominic, I don't want you to go. I couldn't bear loosing you, and besides, since when do you hang out with law enforcement."

"You would be surprised what I do with law enforcement, but I think I need to go and finish this thing. These guys have bothered us for far too long now. We need to lay this to rest."

"Do you think that this is the group that Heinrich was talking about all those years ago? The international leather group that was there to promote our lifestyle?" Dominic asked.

"It certainly might be, but, if it is, they have left some pretty sick and substandard guys into the club. Heinrich would never have approved of what is going on, and, if it is the same club, I doubt that the true leaders would either."

"Do you miss Heinrich, Colin?"

"Every day. Don't you?"

"Well, he was closer to you, and liked you a whole lot better. It's hard to believe that we were his slaves at one point in life. I don't even remember what I was like before our interactions with him. I have to hand it to him, he really taught us a lot, and not just about leather."

"You got that right, Dom. I can't believe that he died, and not of the usual gay thing."

"Whatever happened to his last boy/lover?"

"He's still around. I see him from time to time. Derek is somewhat jealous of him. I think it's because he had a more intense relationship with Heinrich than we are able to have. But then again, Mario didn't really have to work at that time. I don't think that he has ever gotten over that loss. For a while, he was thinking about being a top. He said that he couldn't bear to submit to another man."

"I doubt that lasted very long."

"Well, he and I played after that. He found his inner-slave boy again."

"How touching. We could write a screenplay about it, 'How Mario got his Inner Slave Again'.

"Dominic, I can't believe that you just said that. It was so bad that it doesn't even deserve comment."

By now the two men and two dogs had made a very large circle around their neighborhood. They went back inside and found the rest of the group huddled on a couch; most of them were falling asleep. Colin woke every one up and sent them all to bed. He walked Dominic to the door and kissed him good night. 'Jet lag is a very good thing,' he thought to himself. He turned out the light, petted Finocchio, and went upstairs to join his lovers.

Chapter 17

The next day, Derek was in no mood to do paperwork, or any work for that matter. He went over to the church office and sat at his desk, reading mail and email. When the front door opened, and Millicent eventually walked into his office, he simply couldn't believe his bad luck. He sighed and swallowed hard.

"Hello Bishop, how are you doing today?"

"Oh Derek, could you please call me by my name?"

"Oh, sorry Millicent, how are you doing today?"

"I'm fine. I've received the letter from your vestry, asking me to reconsider the faith rally at St. Peter's. That was very diplomatic of them."

"I'm happy that they were kind to you, but you have to realize that we simply don't tolerate that brand of Christianity here."

"I know. I know that Mark has issues with homosexuality. I thought perhaps that the interaction would cause him to soften a little on his stance."

"I doubt it. He's fairly adamant in his perception of our lifestyle. I guess that the real question here Millicent is, what is your take on the whole thing?"

"I wish that I knew Derek, I wish that I knew. I used to think that I knew. After years in therapy I realized that my animosity toward your relationship was primarily due to jealousy, and then I had to reevaluate the whole thing. I'm not sure where I stand on the issue. And, I'm not sure where I stand on your rather unique relationship, which, even in the gay community, defies most limits."

"I'm sorry about the faith rally, I really am. But are you totally sure of your feelings for this guy? You seem totally smitten by him He's not so friendly to those who disagree with him."

"I'm lonely Derek, and over forty, and a bishop for crying out loud. I can't exactly go out to a singles bar and search for a mate."

"I know. Loneliness is a terrible thing. But it's even a worse motivator."

"I know. But right now I can't discuss it anymore, we have to change the subject. Did you hear about the suicide?"

"What suicide?

"A gay man of a certain age shot himself last night. He must have been a part of your community because they said that he was in bed with books and was wearing a leather harness."

"Who was it?"

"Some man named John Carmichael. The paper wasn't terribly forthcoming with details."

"The name doesn't ring a bell, but he might be someone I've seen from time to time, lurking in the corner of a leather bar."

"Don't even elaborate on that. I have to go to a budget meeting. Thanks for the conversation. We need to do this more often. Believe it or not, I'm not the devil's advocate."

"My dear bishop, shouldn't you be the Lord's advocate?"

"Good bye Derek, take care."

"Good bye Millicent."

As soon as she was gone, Derek was on the phone to Colin. "Hey, do you know a leather man named John Carmichael?"

"No, I don't think so, why?"

"He killed himself last night."

"No, I don't know him."

As the gossip spread around the leather community and the city of Columbus, Joseph and Dave were shocked when they watched the morning news shows and saw a picture of their friend and learned of his fate. They simply couldn't believe that John had committed suicide. Neither one of them thought of him as being particularly depressed; nor did they feel that he gave them any clues that he was about to end his life. Interestingly enough, neither one of them felt any guilt or compunction over the death of their friend.

Billy was at the bookstore, dusting books and arranging CDs for the masses of gay men and women who shopped there. He was scared, and he was depressed that he couldn't seem to get away from the horrible scene that could have ended his life in Pittsburgh. He only felt safe these days with Daniel, Derek, Colin, and Al. Why couldn't he stay in their house all the time? Why did he have to go out to work?

He was worried that Colin would take a job back in Pittsburgh and that Daniel wouldn't want to go along with them. He loved Daniel, and loved being in a relationship with him. But he also loved Colin…deeply. How could he leave the man that had taught him so much? He wondered about all of this while he went about his mindless tasks.

Daniel was a bear at work. He didn't like feeling this way. His home had been violated and his boyfriend was upset. And now, his best friend in the world had the opportunity to leave and go to a different city. Sure, he could go along with them, but what would he do? He wasn't sure how he would even broach the subject with Colin et al, and he wasn't sure if Colin and Derek's offer was just politeness or if they truly wouldn't mind if he and Billy went along.

Al was so happy. He finally completed all of his course work, at least all of the lectures. Now all that he had to do was write the damned paper and get his degree. Oh, and do some sort of internship somewhere. He was happy with Colin and Derek but he wondered if it had been too easy. Should he have tried to get his own relationship before beginning a three-way marriage? Why are these things always so hard? He thought that perhaps he should see a therapist himself. Maybe someone with a fresh perspective could give him a better idea of what was best for him.

Chris was in his apartment, fretting as usual. Nothing seemed to calm him down. He had sex three times in the last twenty-four hours with three different men. He had taken several different kinds of drugs, drank way too much, and generally had become a mess. He really connected with Colin. Why didn't the guy tell him that he had a posse of lovers back at his house? Why had he gotten involved with the far more attractive and alluring Dominic? What was his problem? He knew that there were several issues that he had to resolve in his life, least of which was his own perception of who he was. Oh yeah, he was intelligent, and was completing a graduate degree, and he was attractive, and he was incredibly good in bed, with one of the biggest dicks that he had ever seen, but who was he really?

Dominic was depressed. Of course, he had reasons to be depressed, but if these feelings didn't go away soon, he would have to see someone about it. He missed Amin. At first, he thought that Chris would somehow fill the hole that he felt was left in his heart. He simply couldn't deal with yet another crazy young gay man. And, they weren't exactly compatible in bed—Dominic needed an edge. Colin and the group were great at keeping his mind off of his problems, but he couldn't count on them to be there twenty-four hours a day. As much as he liked the incredibly hot times that they had together, he realized that he needed his own lover, and, sometimes, his own space. His thoughts were disturbed by a knock on the back door. It had to be one of the boys from the group next door.

"Hey cousin, how are you doing?" Colin said, coming into the kitchen.

"I'm not sure," Dominic answered.

"Hey, what's wrong?"

"Oh, you know, the usual...will I ever find love again? Who am I? What's going on? Where am I going?"

"Are you OK? I mean, besides this dramatic summary of your feckless life?"

"Colin, only you could talk to me that way. But I guess that you're right. I'm being a little overly dramatic," Dominic said, sitting down at the kitchen table. At first he started to smile, and then he giggled.

"See, it's not that bad. But now, I'm a little hesitant to tell you what I came over for."

"Let me guess, Patrick from Pittsburgh contacted you."

"Yes, I haven't even told Daniel yet."

"And?"

"Well, he's arranged for a couple of under cover cops to tag Daniel when he pretends to go to the little leather party. You're invited to go along with them."

"Great, when do we leave?"

"You're actually going down first. They are going to wire up Daniel and then put some kind of tracking device in his luggage. He will go to the orgy or whatever, and you will be with these guys and will follow him. After you get there, I'm not sure what you will do. I guess they will decide once they determine what's going on."

"This is all so James Bond, isn't it?"

"Well, of course. We're gay. Want to come over while I tell Daniel, and, even more, when I let Billy know?"

"Let's go. Can I bring Dracul?"

"Of course, he loves to play with Finocchio."

Colin left the house with Dominic and Dracul and made the short trip back to his own place. Of course, the arrival of Colin along with Dominic *and* Dracul warranted an immediate response from Finocchio who barked, and jumped, and ran in circles, and seemed to hop back and forth from man to dog to man. The commotion in the kitchen alerted Al and Derek and the second floor. They came down to see what was going on. By the time that they arrived at the door to the kitchen, Finocchio and Dracul were curled up under the kitchen table.

"What's up?" Derek asked.

"Not anything special, can you call Daniel down here, and you might as well ask Billy to come as well," Colin said.

"What's happened?" Al asked.

Smiling, Colin turned to him and said, "You are such an Italian. Every time someone asks for somebody, you think something is wrong."

"Why are we having a family meeting?" Al continued in his search for what was happening.

"I've heard from the law enforcement people. They are going to help with the leather club event that Daniel has been invited to."

"See, there is something wrong. I knew it," Al answered.

Everyone was kind of laughing at the interaction between Colin and Al when Daniel came down to the kitchen. Daniel was about to breath a sigh of relief thinking that the whole Dark Knights of St. Germaine thing was going to go away quietly. At least, that's what he thought until he saw the look on Al's face. As soon as he saw it, he knew that Colin had heard from his friend in the district attorney's office in Pittsburgh.

"So, what's going to happen to me? Am I going to be put under some sort of cage and lure the evil leather men in?" Daniel joked, mostly to calm his nerves and somewhat to help Billy who had been perpetually distraught since he took the call.

"Not quite that bad. You are going to meet some law enforcement people in Georgia and they will wire you for sound, and attach some sort of homing device to your rental car or in your luggage or something."

"Wow! Isn't this just a little too much like a TV cop show?" Daniel asked.

"Yeah, I know, all of this cloak and dagger stuff, but its there to protect you," Colin answered.

"I don't want you to go," Billy said pleadingly.

"Billy, we have to get to the bottom of this. Daniel is our only true inside connection, although I think that they are playing with him by inviting him. Surely they know that we are all together," Dominic said. "Beside that, I'll be down there with the cops."

"You? Working with the police? That's downright amazing," Derek said with a sneer.

"Well, it's nice to see that the old Derek is back," Dominic teased.

"It's just that I kind of thought that you avoided them as much as possible."

"Look guys, we don't know what 's going to happen down there. Patrick assures me that Daniel will be safe, and that there won't be a moment in time when the police and Dominic aren't within five minutes of being right beside him. I think that we have to trust them on this. I seriously doubt that the entire leather club is out to get us, just a few of the older farts who can't seem to function in the world without a major enemy to focus on. Let's try to see if we can fix this. Unless Daniel himself as some problem. I don't want to force him into anything that he is opposed to," Colin said, trying desperately to calm the group down.

"So, where do we go from here?" Daniel asked.

"Are you willing, and please, if you have reservations, say no," Colin asked.

"I want this stopped, now," Daniel answered.

"Then you have to call Patrick and he will arrange it. You'll have the instructions given to you. Someone from his office will book the reservations for the plane and for the rental car. Prior to leaving the airport, the law enforcement people will meet you—after you go through security, they will wire you up. At that point you will just go there and follow the instructions. You will have to trust that the cops and Dominic will be near you. Here's Patrick's number, don't use a cell phone," Colin said, handing him the piece of paper with the assistant district attorney's number on it.

"How will Dominic get there?" Daniel asked.

"Dom has to call Patrick as well," Colin said.

"Hey, I didn't know that part. He and I don't exactly see eye to eye on most things," Dominic said.

"That was part of the deal, if you want to go. Your reservations and instructions will come through his office. He's going out on a limb here, and he's really only acting as the go-between because essentially he doesn't have any authority here or in Georgia," Colin said.

"Don't you think we need some wine or something?" Al asked.

"Yes, I do – and some snacks, I'm starved," Billy said. "Let me help you."

Billy and Al went into the kitchen while Daniel called Patrick to make the arrangements. After he was finished, Dominic called Patrick as well. Surprisingly enough, the two men were very professional and efficient in making the arrangements. Dominic feared that he would have to eat crow in order to appease Patrick and have him help out with this affair. That didn't happen. By the time that he rejoined the group they were having a nice little wine and cheese party. Who ever said that homosexuals weren't civilized people?

Chapter 18

The next morning, Derek was home alone, sitting at the kitchen table in an old sweatshirt and jeans, eating cereal. The front door bell jarred him from his mindless reverie. When he answered, Millicent was standing on the front porch.

"I know that this is unexpected, but I need to talk," she said, walking through the front door.

"Come on in," Derek deadpanned.

Millicent sat down in the living room, and stared out into space for a few moments. Finally, Derek broke the silence, "Would you like some coffee?"

"Sure."

"I'll go make some."

"I'll come with you. I prefer the kitchen anyway. It's less formal."

As they entered the kitchen, Finocchio took his sentry post under the table. Derek went about making coffee for the two of them, and looking for some rolls or something to have with it.

"You're probably wondering why I'm back here again," Millicent said.

"Is it the faith rally?"

"Not really. It's Mark. Derek, what would you say if I told you that I was thinking about marrying again?"

"Him? You've got to be kidding. By all means Millicent, date him...even have sex with him if you want, but are you sure that you want to marry him? He's rather controversial and would probably alienate you from the community that we call church."

"You're controversial, and yet we seem to have a relationship—granted, it's tense at times, but we're still friends and colleagues."

"I know that, but we're two people. You have many people that you interact with. I'm not so sure how they would feel about it."

"I know. Derek, this is hard. I'm a woman and I don't want to be alone in my life. My marriage to Michael was a mistake, we all know that, but should I have to be alone for the rest of my life because I'm a priest?"

"Well, no. And you're not just a priest; you're a bishop. But when you choose a partner, you're choosing the spouse of a bishop – a public figure, and this guy would have a tremendous amount of baggage coming with him. And I doubt that he would tolerate your friends, me being the biggest example of that. And how would you handle it when he denounces my kind and me from his pulpit? And where would you worship?"

"Trust me, Derek. I've thought of all of those questions and more. I just seem to be mesmerized by this man. Maybe I've been alone for too long."

"Have you spoken with your counselors, Millicent?"

"I'm about to do that today. I just needed some moral support from you first."

"Have you spoken to him about your concerns? And, forgive this question, are you two romantically involved or are you thinking ahead again?"

"We've been sort of dating, I think."

"And you've brought up your position as bishop with him?"

"Well, he doesn't believe in bishops."

"Millicent, believe or not, you're a reality and part of that reality is that you are a bishop. He has to see that."

"I know, I know. But thanks for listening. How have you been? What have you been up to?"

"I'm at loose ends with myself. My relationship is good; Colin and Al are great. It's fun living in a house with Billy and Daniel upstairs, but I'm restless."

"Do you want to move on to a different church?"

"I'm not sure. I want to stay in this relationship, but I'm not so sure about the priesthood thing. It's not that I think that gay men can't be priests, but it's where my attention is focused. I'm asking myself, should I devote more time to this relationship and all that it would entail, or should I kind of be half and half—priest at times, and a devoted follower of my baser instincts."

“I’ve never understood those, Derek. I’ve only accepted them because I have accepted you as a friend. I don’t have problems with gay people. Heaven knows I couldn’t be a bishop in the Episcopal Church if I did, but it’s the leather thing that I will never understand.”

“Don’t worry. Many gay men don’t understand it either. Sometimes, those involved with it don’t understand it even while we’re in the midst of it.”

“As long as you’re happy and it doesn’t hurt anyone…”

“Well, hurt is sometimes a big part of it,” Derek said and started to chuckle.

“Oh you! I have to go. Thanks for the coffee and the friendly words.

Derek showed Millicent to the door and, after he closed it, he looked at Finocchio and said, “We aren’t doing anything today.” He went upstairs, took a long shower and called Colin.

“I’m staying home today and doing nothing.”

“Good for you—I’ll be done here shortly if you need anything,” Colin said.

“Nope. Don’t think that I need anything. I don’t want to cook tonight. And I think that Billy and Daniel should be alone tonight—he’s going off to Georgia in a couple of days and they should spend some time alone.”

Colin could read between the lines. Derek may have Daniel and Billy’s best interests at heart, but he also wanted to be alone with Al and him tonight. It had been a long time since they spent an entire evening at home alone. Once he got off the phone with Derek, he called Al and the two of them cooked up a plan for the evening. Then he called Daniel and told him that he and Billy should spend a little time alone tonight—and said that Derek needed some time alone as well.

Later that day, Colin picked up Al on campus and they drove to the local gay bookstore. Billy was working, or, at least he was doing what he passed off as working. Al browsed through the books, CDs and DVDs to find some things for all of them to watch, listen to, or read for the evening. It had begun to snow—winter was late to arrive this year but it was determined to stay on for as long as possible. Colin was talking to Billy.

"Billy, you and Daniel are spending tonight alone. Derek needs some time alone with us and I think that Daniel needs some time alone with you."

"Yeah, you're probably right. I'm not thrilled about this whole thing, you know."

"I know. He'll be all right."

"You can say that – you've never experienced these guys. I have twice."

"And the reason that we're all doing this is so you never have to experience it again."

Al came up to the counter and paid for the books and DVDs that he had picked out. They stopped at the florist shop, a bakery, and then called ahead and ordered the really good Chinese food that Derek liked. On the way there, they stopped and picked out a couple of very good bottles of wine. By the time that they arrived home, they were laden with packages. The house was quiet except for the thump, thump of Finocchio's tail under the kitchen table. Colin and Al worked quietly, arranging the flowers, lighting candles, and setting the kitchen table. Beside Derek's place, they put a couple of books and the DVDs that they planned on watching. Al put the Chinese food in attractive serving dishes while Colin went upstairs to get Derek, who he found asleep on the bed.

"Hey there, little one. Want some dinner?" he said as he slipped his arm around Derek's neck.

"What? What time is it?"

"It's almost four o'clock and I know that it's early, but I thought that you might have forgone lunch. I had a feeling that you would be napping today."

"Ummmm...yes, and it felt great. What's for dinner?"

"It's a surprise, come on downstairs. By the way, it's snowing out."

"I hate winter," Derek said, getting out of bed.

"You love winter," Colin countered.

"OK, I love winter. In books."

They went down the back stairs that led directly into the kitchen. It was a cozy scene with candlelight, soft music playing and the smell of Chinese food. There were wine glasses filled with wine and several bottles waiting to be opened. Derek sat down at his place and picked up the packages. "What's this?"

"Some entertainment for this evening," Al said.

"I must be getting old. Entertainment used to mean whips and restraints."

"Well, that could happen, but I think that you need tonight to rest."

"I rest a lot, you know."

The men started off the dinner quietly, but by then end of the first bottle of wine they were talking about everything and about nothing. The food was good and the snow didn't appear to be letting up. What Derek didn't know at that point was that Colin and Al had already decided to spend tomorrow at home. Amazing how an at-home day was contagious. One person in a household does it and the next thing you know, everyone else was doing it as well.

Desert that night was from the Austrian bakery that Colin loved. The meal was good and Al and Derek offered to clean up the kitchen while Colin took a shower. Finocchio wasn't too pleased. Chinese food wasn't his favorite cuisine; he did like the fortune cookies, but he preferred it when the men ate Italian or, even better, when they had meat. That night they watched movies and read books, all curled up on the bed with Finocchio—he *did* like that part of it. Before turning out the lights, Colin heard Daniel and Billy quietly walking up the stairs to their apartment. He turned off the alarm clock and then shut off the lights.

He was frantically awoken by Derek the next morning at seven. "Hey, what's up, aren't you getting ready for work?"

"Don't worry, Al and I took today off," Colin said sleepily.

"Hey, I'm the only one that usually does that. You should see it outside. It really snowed a lot."

"Did it stop?" Al asked, waking up.

"Mostly. I mean it still looks like its flurries out there, but it's amazing how much it snowed. I don't know if Daniel will be able to get out tomorrow."

"Derek. Airports may close for a few hours, or even a day – but it will be back open tomorrow. Did it shut down?" Colin asked.

"I don't really know. I just assumed that it did."

Later that morning, as Colin, Al, and Derek padded around the house doing nothing in particular, Billy sneaked down the stairs...

"Am I allowed in again?" he asked.

Derek threw a pillow at him and Al ran over to tackle him. "Hey, what's up with you old guys? Did somebody put Geritol in your cereal this morning? Why are all of you home today?"

"We took the day off. Snow day," Colin answered as Billy crawled into bed beside him and curled up in his arms.

"Hey catamite, that's my man," Derek said.

"You guys are all in such good moods. Don't you know that Daniel is going into the lion's den tomorrow?"

Derek was speechless. He knew that Billy was bright and well educated. What he always forgot was that he could be clever and witty at times. "That was pretty good for you, Billy," he said.

"I'm really worried about him," Billy said.

"We all are, Billy," Colin assured him.

"Are we banned from dinner tonight as well?"

"No — we're having dinner together. All of us are having dinner together, including Dominic.

That night, the six of them gathered for a very subdued dinner. No one was saying the obvious, that they were scared of what was about to happen the next day. It was cozy in the kitchen and very cold outside, with light snow falling, making the neighborhood seem like a fantasy world. Both dogs were under the kitchen table, basking in the heat of the oven.

"So, tomorrow's the big day?" Al asked.

"Yeah – a very big day. I'm not sure what's going to happen," Daniel answered.

"Boys, we can't dwell on this too much. It will drive us crazy. We just have to trust that everything will work out. We don't even know if these guys are the ones that have been causing all of the trouble. After all, this is supposed to be a pretty big group," Dominic continued.

"Colin, tell me more about Heinrich. Didn't he belong to an international leather group?" Derek asked.

Colin looked at Dominic, who looked right back at him. Both men were thinking the same thing that Derek was beginning to feel. Neither one of them had any concrete evidence that Heinrich belonged to the same group, but the evidence, coincidental though it may be, seemed to be weighing heavily that it was. Colin had already decided that Heinrich would never have been involved in such a horrible thing as what had been happening here in America. He decided to be forthcoming. "What do you want to know?"

"Who was he? What were you to him? How did you meet? Was he involved in something like this?" Derek continued.

"Well, as you know, it was some time ago. Heinrich found me outside a leather bar in San Francisco. I had just been thrown out. Of course, I was wearing a teal colored alligator shirt, jeans, white tennis shoes and about a half a bottle of *Aramis* cologne."

"You're kidding me? You, dressed like that? In a leather bar?" Billy asked incredulously.

"I told you, it was a long time ago. Anyway, I was asked to leave—*sternly* asked to leave and given assistance to achieve that end. Heinrich was about thirty-five at the time—I was only twenty-two. He came out, very hot in his full leather, with that German accent and asked if I needed some help. I was a little put off by the whole thing and said no, and then go fuck yourself. I got up and left."

"Well, that was an auspicious beginning," Daniel chuckled.

"The next time that I saw Heinrich was in a leather bar in Chicago. Again, I was thrown out. This time I had a beautiful leather jacket and black boots, but I hadn't learned to loose the cologne yet. He took pity on me and said that he could help me improve my image with the leather set. He lived in DC at the time and I was in Philadelphia, so it was kind of close by. He told me that he would teach me everything that he knew, but that I would have to do exactly what he said and that I would have to call him Sir. He alluded to the fact that I would be his slave for at least a year."

"You didn't do it, did you?" Billy asked. "You were never a slave to anyone were you?"

"Yes, I was. Not totally willingly, but I wanted to be like him in the bar and was willing to go through anything to get to that point. So, I became his slave. He was generous. Much of the time we would go traveling; New York, Chicago, San Francisco, and many trips to Germany and Amsterdam. He did to me what I've done to many of you, and more. And yes, I serviced his friends as well."

"It was at this time that I wanted to be involved with it as well, and joined Colin with Heinrich and started the same process,"

Dominic added.

"So, you two were with him for a year and then, poof, he made you a leather man?" Al asked.

"Remember, Heinrich was German. Everything had to do with protocol and ceremony. There was what could only be called an initiation scene in Germany that I remember to this day. It took place on Walpurgistnacht, which is April 30th and has some significance in the German Gnostic world. It was a very hot scene, and, at the end, I was presented with my leather – some of which I wear to this day."

"And what happened to Heinrich?" Billy asked.

"He died. And not of what everyone else died of at the time. As a matter of fact, we didn't know for a while. He went off by himself, abandoned his lover/slave, and we all found out about it a little later."

"Why did he do that?" Derek asked.

"No one knows for sure."

"And what happened to his lover?" Daniel asked.

"He's still around. A very handsome man—hot actually. I talk to him from time to time. And Dominic knows him."

"So, was he involved in the Dark Knights of St. Germaine?" Daniel asked.

"That's the part that I'm not so sure about. Heinrich was very intelligent, with several graduate degrees. And he was accomplished, and rich. I know that he was involved in Druidism and the Knights Templar, but I don't know how much. And I don't know what leather organizations he belonged to. But I can tell you this much, whatever he was involved in, it didn't involve permanent harm to anyone. And, if he didn't like you, he simply ignored you."

"So you think that this group is different?" Daniel asked.

"I'm not sure. But I do know that it has some elements in it that managed to get there without going through the proper steps. And, any European group would rid itself of them if they had a clue what was going on?"

"How could they not know?" Billy asked.

"Remember, the USA is important to us, and we know everything that goes on. For crying out loud, there can be a car chase in Wyoming and it's on the national news that day. But in

Europe, they might not be paying attention to our goings on in this country. Dominic, what do you think?"

"I agree with you Colin. Our goal, once we take care of the problem at hand, is to inform the group in Europe what's going on. I have a feeling that it has to do with what we've seen in leather clubs all across the country. You get a couple of men that have no real life outside the leather club and they make it their life's work to insure that *they* are the defining authority in the club. That's why I've shied away from them my whole life. I tried joining one once and all they talked about in meetings was how much money they made doing this, and where they would go for some lame demonstration. I don't think that the group had real sex at any time."

"There are some good ones, but you have to watch out, especially in the provinces," Colin continued. "And when it comes to leather…Columbus, Pittsburgh, and Philadelphia, for that matter, are definitely the provinces.

"Wow! It's getting late," Billy said.

Everyone looked at him. He was clearly the youngest person in the room and it was only approaching ten o'clock. At first, people thought that he was joking and then it dawned on each one of them. He wanted to be with Daniel, alone. And knowing Billy, he probably wanted to have sex with him before they parted for Daniel's great adventure the next day.

Colin walked Dominic to the door. As he said goodbye, he asked, "Have you heard from Chris lately?"

"No, but I could swear that I saw him driving by one day. And I didn't think that he had a car."

"I'm not so sure it's over with him. I really wish one of us had stayed in touch with him. I think he needs help."

"Well, let's deal with one problem at a time, Colin."

Colin locked the doors, patted Finocchio on the head and went upstairs. Derek and Al were in bed, reading. At some point that night they had an intimate encounter and went to sleep. It wasn't really sex, but, then again, it wasn't 'not-sex' either. It was one of those times when the intimacy of the relationship took over for the intensity of the act.

Chapter 19

The next morning, Dominic and Daniel drove to the airport. They parted once inside, each of them was taking a separate flight to their destination. They did this just in case there was someone watching them on the flight down to the south. Once there, Daniel had his instructions and would follow them exactly. Well, he had two sets of instructions, the ones given to him by the mysterious voice on the phone and the other, from the equally mysterious law enforcement group that Colin had him contact. Dominic was meeting the two officers at a designated meeting point that Patrick had given him over the phone. There was a break in the weather that morning so the flights went off as scheduled.

Back at the house, there were four men staying home and worrying about the fate of their friend and, in Billy's case, lover. Interestingly enough, each man had his own way of dealing with the stress and worry over their friends' fates. Derek went down to clean the dungeon and spruce it up. Billy stayed on his floor and cleaned, and then cleaned again. Al went to the store and started cooking for what seemed to be an army, while Colin listened to music and read.

Dominic arrived in Georgia first. He went to the designated meeting place and met the two very hot cops. He couldn't believe how incredibly attractive both of them were. As a matter of fact, for the first time in his life, he regretted his mode of living and his connection with groups that would put him on the opposing side of law enforcement.

"Hello Dominic, my name is Gary and this is Paul, my partner," the first cop said.

"How did you know who I am?" Dominic asked.

"We have our ways," Paul said and all three men started laughing. They shook hands and Gary explained what was about to happen.

"We've arranged with the rental car agency for Daniel to get a specific car. Another officer will meet him in the airport and will check his wire, just to make sure that it's working. We won't be far from the rental car agency, and we will start to track the car as soon as he gives us the word. We will follow him to the designated location and we will observe what is going on."

"How will we do that unseen?" Dominic asked.

"Again Dominic, we have our ways, you'll have to trust us," Paul said, placing a hand on Dominic's shoulder. This simple act caused such a stir in Dominic's groin; he couldn't believe that it was happening.

Meanwhile, Daniel managed to meet his connection at the airport and found his way to the car rental place. He was somewhat skeptical about being backed up in this endeavor, his last experience with the leather club wasn't so great, but he decided to trust everyone on this matter. He desperately wanted this whole chapter in his life to end so he could get on with Billy.

Once he was in the car, he simply said the words, 'the eagle has landed', and started off. The directions were specific, but it was mid-afternoon in the middle of winter, so he was concerned that he would get lost. Of course, he shouldn't have cared if he got lost, the police would find him; but then again, he would have ruined the whole purpose of this trip. It wasn't long before Daniel found the turn off specified in the directions, and, shortly after that, the fence that he needed to open.

Once he closed the fence, he continued down a dirt road to what he thought appeared to be some sort of militia camp. Actually, it was a section of a farm that had once housed a summer camp for boys. That was many years ago. Now there were cabins with a central main 'lodge' and several interesting paths and small bridges and campfire sites. Daniel could see several tents that had been set up and a flurry of activity around the lodge. What he couldn't see, was Dominic along with the two cops parking way down the road before the turnoff, and them sneaking through the woods in camouflage outfits.

Back in Columbus the four men in Colin's house had settled into an uneasy kind of routine. Al's dinner that night was an experience in excess, and the men ate, and drank, well. They all agreed to watch a movie together after cleaning up and walking the two dogs. Two dogs required four men to walk them and so they got into their best 'gay men walking dogs in the winter' clothes and set out for what they hoped would be a quick walk around the neighborhood.

As they walked up the street, passed Dominic's house, Lee and Michael were driving up. There was a third man with them and, once they got out of the car, it was apparent that they had availed themselves of happy hour at some bar and were coming home with a third to liven their evening. The third man happened to be Chris. As soon as he saw him, Colin tensed up, which in turn, caused the dogs to bark. Of course, Lee and Michael had no compunction about saying hello to the boys, but this simply did not go well with Chris.

"What are you doing here?" the Italian boy yelled.

"Chris, I live here," Colin answered.

"You live with these two guys...and those guys? Do you fuck every one in this town?" Chris continued to yell.

Colin walked over to Chris to try to bring the entire interaction down a notch or two. As he grabbed Chris's arm, the Italian started yelling that he was being attacked. This, in turn, caused the dog to try to protect Colin. Dracul was not a small dog and soon the altercation reached a level that, in other circumstances, would look like something out of a Gilbert and Sullivan opera. However, the police in the cruiser coming down the street didn't quite see it that way. Within minutes, they were out, guns drawn, ordering all the parties to separate.

"That man is involved with some sick ritualistic cult where he imprisons and tortures people," Chris said, pointing at Colin.

"Oh, for crying out loud Chris, you've never been in my house. I don't have a cult, I don't have anything..." Colin was trying to say.

"Everybody shut up," the younger of the two cops said.

Within a few minutes, Chris had convinced the two policemen that Colin had attacked him and had trained the dog on him. Not wanting to spend a night in the cold trying to sort through the whole thing, the police decided to arrest Colin and let a judge decide what had been going on that night. He was placed in handcuffs, taken to the car, and was then transported to the police station. All of the men left on the street were in shock, except for Chris who kept shouting that someone had to take him back to his neighborhood.

Colin endured the humiliation of being taken to a jail cell, finger printed, and having mug shots taken. After what seemed to be an eternity he finally appeared before a rather tired looking night court judge who let him go on his own recognizance and ordered him back to court for a hearing the following week. When he came out of the small courtroom, he found Derek waiting for him. Al had stayed with Billy who was already nervous about being alone with Daniel out of town.

"I can't believe this," Colin said as he embraced Derek.

"Do you need a lawyer or bail money?" Derek asked.

"No, but I have to come back and answer to these charges next week. This is appalling."

"Well, there are five of us who will testify that you weren't assaulting that man," Derek said, trying to comfort Colin.

When they got back to the house they found that Al and Billy were pacing back and forth in the front hallway. The police had arrived with a search warrant and were taking several pictures of the basement dungeon. Apparently the police felt that Chris's accusations about a dungeon were sufficient to order an investigation. They finished up and came back upstairs.

"Do I have to go with you again officers?" Colin asked.

"No, but it doesn't look good down there, sir," the younger one answered.

The conversation ended there and the police excused themselves. All of the men were simply too shocked to say or do anything. Colin didn't want to talk, he didn't want to drink, he didn't want to do anything except be alone. Derek had never seen Colin so upset about anything. He wanted to comfort Colin but simply didn't know how to do it.

Back in Georgia, Dominic and his two sidekicks, Gary and Paul, managed to sneak into the camp. They blended in sufficiently well not to cause any alarm. Apparently militia outfits passed for the uniform of the day in this camp. They stayed on the periphery, out of site of the majority of the men there.

Daniel, on the other hand, had checked into a cabin and had already unpacked. As he put on his leathers, a knock came at the door.

"Daniel, we're so glad that you could come," Joseph said.

"Thank you, but I'm not sure that I know you, and I didn't think that we were supposed to use names here."

"Oh, we're almost old friends," Joseph continued.

Daniel, to his credit, kept his unease at bay and continued on with Joseph, "When do the festivities start?"

"Very soon, you should be getting out to the center of the compound."

"Let me just get situated here and I'll be right out."

Joseph left Daniel in his cabin. As soon as the door was shut, he breathed a heavy sigh. This was going to be hard. To himself, and his little wire, he said quietly, 'I hope you guys are somewhere here.' Then he went out to join the group for the initiation. Initiations were big in this club—they didn't happen often and everyone seemed to show up for them. He was reminded of his own initiation. Of course then, he had an entirely different view of this club. So much had changed since that night. He was so happy that he met Billy, and Colin, and Derek, and Al, and Dominic. They had become so much a part of his life. He *hoped* that he would be able to see them again.

As he walked to the center of the camp, he was shocked to see that the man hanging from the cross was wearing a leather executioner's hood. That was so unlike any of the other initiations that he had witnessed. But he hadn't been to that many, so perhaps this was what happened at times. As the ceremony progressed, there was something oddly familiar about the man; just something in the way that he spoke and carried himself. After the formal part of the initiation was over, the orgy began. It was at this point that Daniel froze. He looked across the area and saw Dave—the man who had been with Ben when Amin and Billy were being tortured.

Dave knew enough to keep a certain distance between him and Daniel at this point. His revenge would come a little later. He and Joseph would take care of that, but there was certainly time for that to happen later tonight. For right now, he would participate in the orgy going on in the compound. There was a hot leather boy over on the other side that he wanted to tie up and flog.

On the periphery of the camp, Gary, Paul, and Dominic were

watching what was going on. Daniel noticed Dave as well, and pointed him out to the two cops, letting them know that he was at least present when Amin met his fate at their hands.

"When are we going to make our move?" he asked the two cops.

"I'm not sure. Granted, this is a little weird for me, but I'm not so sure that we've seen any major laws broken tonight, yet," Gary answered.

"I think maybe we could just raid the place. Call the local state police and have them come down and at least give everybody a scare," Paul added.

"That's just what I didn't want to happen. I don't want this to be just another form of police and state oppression for my community. I mean, there are a couple of these guys that I really don't like, but I don't want everyone to suffer because of it," Dominic said.

"Hey, I'm on your side. And I'm just as gay as you are," Paul said. "But I'm not sure how we should proceed here. And I think that we're going to need some help when we do make our move. There are a lot of guys here. We're definitely outnumbered."

Back in Columbus, Colin had finally settled down. He had spoken to his attorney who felt that this whole thing would simply be an irritation. At least, that was his hope. When you're gay in America these days, you never knew. The simple things in life could turn into a major event. While his attorney did a lot to put his mind at ease, Colin still carried that uneasy feeling in the back of his mind. Al and Derek had given up trying to console him and had gone to bed. Billy, on the other hand, stayed up with Colin. It was most assuredly a case of misery loves company.

"Do you think Daniel and Dominic are OK?" Billy asked.

"I'm sure that they are. The police are with them. Nothing is going to happen to any of them."

"Colin, I've known you for a long time now, and I've been involved in leather. This is just too unreal. I didn't think that this stuff happened. Not even in badly written novels."

"Billy, it generally doesn't happen *except* in badly written novels. But it seems to have happened here."

"When do you think that they will be back?"

"I'm sure that they will be here tomorrow. And we might even find that we've had more excitement than they did," Colin answered, knowing full well, given the history with this group that he was probably misleading Billy. "Come over here."

Billy scooted over to Colin on the couch and the two men embraced, kissing each other passionately. Within a couple of minutes, their clothes were off and they were all over each other. Colin did something that he rarely did – he started to suck Billy's cock. It didn't take long for the young man to cum. Colin reached up and kissed Billy, who could now taste his own cum on Colin's lips. In a couple of minutes he returned the favor and the two of them fell into a fitful sleep together.

Somewhere in the forests of Georgia, Daniel was not comfortably falling asleep with someone he cared about. He was out in the cold winter night watching a whole bunch of men either having or trying to have sex with each other. Half of them were attractive, and half of them had really let themselves go. He wished that he could be back in the relative comfort and calm of the house back in Columbus.

Joseph and Dave were taking a break from the festivities, discussing what to do with Daniel and the every perplexing problem of Billy. "Well, we could give him a good scare down here and insure that he keeps quiet," Joseph said.

"But we don't really want to hurt him, do we?" Dave asked.

"Not intentionally, but if something happens, I certainly can't be held responsible."

"We can't have that happen at one of these gatherings," Dave added. "There are too many things that have happened with our members being involved.

"Who says that it has to happen while everyone is here. We could stay behind tomorrow and show him what we can do. Yes, yes, we won't intentionally harm him, but, if he suffers some ill after we leave, can we be held accountable? And, even if we can, who will know that it's us. He's been to these things before."

"What do you have in mind?" Dave asked.

"Let's start by hooding him, gagging him, and tying him up out in the woods."

Back at the periphery of the camp, Dominic and his cop friends were becoming impatient while they waited for their chance.

Gary had already called for some backup and the Georgia troopers would be standing by, ready to help in the eventuality that they were needed. This made Paul a little nervous, but he trusted the system and hoped that this wouldn't turn into some kind of antigay circus.

"When do you think they will do anything?" Paul asked.

"I doubt that they would do anything while everyone is around. I really don't think that everyone here is as nefarious as the few that have been causing all the problems back at home," Dominic added.

"It's cold out here," Paul said.

"You could come a little closer, if you'd like," Dominic said, inviting Paul to come nearer to him.

"Would you guys cut it out? You can both get a room after this is over," Gary chided.

Just as they were joking around a little bit, they could here voices talking to Daniel. They could see a couple of men walking with Daniel, much like old friends who have become bored at some venue, and were take a breather from the crowds. As soon as they disappeared behind some trees, all three men of them became a little anxious. Soon, they heard the two older sounding voices attempting to rough up Daniel who was protesting, and then simply grunting. It was clear that he was being dragged.

"Want to try to handle this ourselves?" Gary asked.

"No, there are too many people here. The crowd mentality may take over and then we're doomed," Paul said.

"Come on guys, hurry up, Daniel may be in trouble," Dominic said, getting up.

As Gary called for the backup to come into the camp, he got up, along with Paul and Dominic and crossed the clearing and went into the trees where they saw the two men walking with Daniel. As they walked faster into the forest, Paul and Gary drew their weapons. What they didn't expect was for Dominic to pull out a gun as well.

"Are you licensed to carry that?" Gary asked.

"Do you really think that this is the time to ask that question?" Paul added. "We can use all of the help that we can get."

As they got further into the forest, they could hear Joseph and Dave struggling with Daniel. They could also hear the initial stages of the state troopers invasion into the camp. They came to a small clearing and saw Joseph and Dave struggling with rope. Daniel had a gag in his mouth and they were about to tie him to a tree. Gary and Paul motioned for Dominic to be quiet—they were trying to see if either of the older men had a weapon that they could use on Daniel. Joseph started to rip open Daniel's jacket and got tripped up in the wires.

"What the hell is this? You some kind of electro-bottom-freak?" Joseph sneered. He didn't recognize the wire for what it was.

It was at that precise moment that Gary, Paul, and Dominic rushed the threesome, with Gary holding out a badge while Paul aimed his weapon. "Stop—police!" Paul yelled. The two older men didn't quite know what to do. They weren't quite sure that this wasn't some sort of scene orchestrated by the leather club. That is, they weren't sure until Dave saw Dominic's face and recognized him as the lover of the man that Ben had tortured so cruelly. Both Joseph and Dave put their hands in the air. Dominic went over to Daniel and undid the gag, the blindfold, and the ropes.

"Were you hurt? Are you all right?" Dominic asked.

"Just a little uneasy about these two, I'm sure that they were involved with Billy and Amin the last time," Daniel said.

Dominic turned around and while Gary and Paul were busy handcuffing the two older men, he made a fist and punched Dave squarely in the mouth. The older man went sailing backwards. Paul pushed Dominic back and told him to control himself, although he wasn't particularly upset at what had happened. As they were finishing up, two state troopers came into the clearing and shined their flashlights on them, shouting, "Stop! Police! Don't move!"

Gary and Paul said in unison, "We're the guys who called you," and, flashed the troopers their badge. It didn't take long for the troopers to discover which of the men were the bad guys and which ones were the good guys. As they were walking back toward the camp, they could see a whole bunch of troopers and a lot of leather men looking rather sheepish as bright lights and men in uniforms who looked like they meant business surrounded them.

Confusion reined supreme that night. Each man was taken to an area and questioned as to the reason that he was there. Most of the men knew nothing about the murders in Pittsburgh or West

Virginia, and almost none of them knew who Billy was or Daniel, for that matter. One man in particular gave the police a hard time. Interestingly enough, he was very near the last to be questioned.

"Sir, you will have to take off that hat, or whatever it is," the agent said.

"I would rather not," the man replied.

"Well, let's see. You can do it now, or you can do it in jail."

"I don't see what I've done wrong, officer."

"You are not listening to law enforcement in the investigation of a crime scene. Now, remove it."

The policeman couldn't believe his luck. Why did he have to get this assignment tonight, and why this crazy man who insisted on wearing a mask right out of a mediaeval movie. The officer looked up at the man who was now looking down.

"I take it that you have retrieved your personal belongings. I will need some form of identification with a picture and your home address on it."

"Really officer, I don't see the point. I've cooperated so far, why can't I simply go home. I really don't know anything about what is going on. Why should I be subjected to this? Is gathering in the forest a crime?"

"Well, now, let's see. There were several men tied up. There were several men being tortured. There may very well have been crimes taking place here, but we are here to investigate another crime and, if you make it a little easier on us, we may forget the crimes that we've already seen."

The officer took the driver's license and started to write down the information. Mark Marjoram...Columbus, Ohio. He handed the card back to Mark who sat there, stunned.

The policeman continued to fill out paperwork and asked Mark several questions. After a few minutes, he said, "Well Mr. Marjoram, it appears that you don't know anything about the murders that have taken place, so we're going to let you go home. I would suggest that you don't do this sort of thing again, unless you're in the privacy of your own home, and then, I have to warn you, if there would be a complaint, we would arrest you for that."

Mark was simply glad to be finished with the officials in this horrible moment in his life. His whole reputation, not to mention, his livelihood could have been jeopardized by tonight. He will definitely not be doing this any time in the near future. He was gathering the stuff that he had in his cabin and was heading back up the dirt road to where all the cars were. Of course there were a million lights up there. Why did the police always have to make such a production out of these things? As he was walking up the road, he passed four men standing by a late model car. They were all very attractive, and two of them were cops. He wondered if the other two were still being questioned. When he turned the bend in the road he was greeted by the flashing of cameras and several news people holding video cameras. One person was holding a microphone, speaking to a cameraman. Of course, it was a national news station. Well, he was sure that no one would know him dressed like he was. As he continued walking, the astute newscaster turned aside and said, “Ladies and gentlemen, we have a celebrity here tonight. Rev. Mark Marjoram, how did you come to be here?”

Mark ran to his car. How could anyone have recognized him in the dark in the middle of the woods in Georgia? He couldn’t believe it. He knew what would happen next. They would be checking records and cross checking with the lists that the police had prepared. Why were the cops always in bed with news teams? He got into his car and sped away into the night.

Back down the road, Dominic was comforting Daniel, while Paul and Gary looked on. “I just want to go home,” Daniel said.

“Don’t worry, we have a flight very soon, if the police are finished with us,” Dominic said.

“Well, kind of. We will need you to testify, both of you. Daniel for tonight, and Dominic, you for the events that happened in West Virginia. So, we will be in touch with both of you,” Paul said.

“I think that I would like that,” Dominic replied.

“I can’t believe you guys. We’re here with a bunch of weirdoes in cow hide and you two are setting up a date,” Gary joked.

“Hey, I happen to be one of those weirdoes myself,” Dominic said.

“So, you live in Columbus?” Paul asked Dominic.

“Yeah, and where do you live, officer?” Dominic asked.

“Well, it’s special agent, and I live in Pittsburgh, but I might have to rethink that,” Paul replied.

"Don't worry—the two cities aren't terribly far apart. But right now, Daniel and I need some transportation back to the airport. Can you help us out?"

"Already taken care of. Gary, can you get a ride with someone?" Paul asked.

"Always dropped as soon as some pretty gay boy comes by," Gary continued on in his relentless teasing of Paul.

It was extremely early in the morning when Dominic and Daniel landed in Columbus. It must have snowed the whole time that they were in Georgia. The place was a winter wonderland and they had to spend quite a bit of time cleaning off the car. It was about six o'clock in the morning when they got back to their street and into Daniel's house. There, in the living room, Billy and Colin were curled up in a ball, sleeping soundly. There wasn't anyone stirring in the house at all; it was totally silent, except for the thump, thump, thump of Finocchio's tail in the kitchen.

"It's nice to see that your lover took solace in the arms of another man while you were out risking your life," Dominic teased Daniel.

"That's one relationship that no one will ever come between, or understand for that matter. Let's wake them up and all go to bed. I need a shower. You staying over here?"

"Yeah, I think that I will."

Chapter 20

The next morning was a total flurry of activity. Derek and Al woke to find Colin and Dominic in their bed. They assumed that Daniel was upstairs with Billy. They couldn't contain themselves for long. "Hey, wake up. What happened? Is everything OK?" Derek said, shaking Colin.

"Don't you ever sleep, Derek" Dominic said groggily.

"Tell us what happened," Al said.

Both Colin and Dominic got up after only a couple hours sleep. "Go up and wake Billy and Daniel, come downstairs and we'll make breakfast. I'll tell you the whole thing then," Dominic said.

Soon there were six men sitting around the kitchen table. Dracul came up from the basement to join Finocchio under the table. Al was making pancakes for the group and Daniel was retelling the story of what happened in Georgia. Dominic would add small bits of information for clarification when he thought that it was needed. After everyone felt that they were up to date on those activities, the conversation turned to the events in Columbus.

"I should have threatened that little Italian when I had the chance," Dominic said.

"Oh great, just what I need, a new charge added to what is probably waiting for me on Monday," Colin said into his plate of pancakes.

"I can't believe it, what's wrong with that kid," Dominic continued.

The men fell silent. Derek got up to turn on the morning news shows to see if it was going to snow again today in Columbus. It came on just as the newscaster said, "And when we come back, a local celebrity is caught with his pants down, literally, in the woods in Georgia. You won't believe who it is...when we return." The news then cut to commercial.

Colin turned to Daniel, "Are you a celebrity?"

"I don't think so, and my pants were never down," Daniel answered.

"Are you sure about that?" Billy asked.

"I am, how about yours?" Daniel continued, teasing. Well, half teasing anyway.

The news came back on, introducing a clip from some film shot in Georgia where, according to the newscaster, homosexual men had gathered for a ceremony involving sadomasochistic activity that included beatings, bondage, and things that wouldn't be fit for the morning news. When they ran the film, there was Mark Marjoram, looking very guilty in the Georgia night. The newscaster continued, "The Reverend Mark Marjoram was asked for a comment on his presence at this gathering. He declined, and sped off into the night." The anchor's partner added, "Perhaps to give someone else his spiritual guidance." And then the news continued with other stories.

"I can't believe it," Derek exclaimed. "I couldn't have asked for anything better."

"Isn't that the guy that your Bishop is in love with?" Billy asked.

"It most certainly is. I wonder how this will affect her," Derek answered.

"Well, besides us, does anyone else know of her dalliance with the man?" Colin asked.

"Umm...let's see, the bishop's counselors, the standing committee, a few people that have seen them at restaurants, us, and all the people that we've told...no, only a few hundred or so. I wonder if she has seen it yet, I should call her."

"Why don't you wait until a civilized hour, like noon," Al suggested.

"Why? So she could legitimately have a cocktail then?" Derek joked.

"She will be completely devastated—not to mention that she might be totally humiliated as well," Al continued.

"I always said, beware of those Christians, they'll get you every time," Colin added. "But the question remains, will she be more humiliated than I once I appear in court to answer charges of assaulting a graduate student from another country and having pictures of my dungeon available for all to see."

"Well, you should be happy, I did clean it before they got here," Derek said. "Besides, since when are you upset about having your sex life paraded around in public?"

"When I'm doing the parading, I don't mind, but when it's paraded for me, I get a little uncomfortable."

"You are taking an attorney with you, aren't you?" Dominic asked.

"Not only an attorney, but all of these guys and Lee and Michael as well. They are going to be my witnesses that I didn't really attack Chris."

"This is such a tremendous pain in the ass," Dominic said.

"Tell me about it – it's my ass that has the pain in it."

After breakfast, Dominic and Daniel returned to bed, to sleep. Al went off to school to pick up papers and check on things in his graduate student office. Billy and Colin decided to watch a movie on the television in the library on the second floor. Derek went over to the church office to call Millicent.

"Hello, Bishop Barclay," Millicent answered.

"Millicent, it's Derek."

"I assume that you've heard, or seen, what has happened," she said with a sigh.

"I did. Actually, all of us were peripherally involved in what was going on down there. Apparently that group had a few bad apples in it, one of whom committed the murder in Pittsburgh and one who was present when they got a little out of hand with Billy and Amin. But, right now, that's beside the point. How are you?"

"Waiting for the other shoe to fall. I haven't heard from anyone yet, but I'm sure that I will."

"I take it that you spoke to people about your relationship?"

"Right after I spoke with you the other day. I wish I had taken your advice and waited around to see if things were going to work out. But now, I think I have to face the humiliation that I used significantly bad judgment in my personal life."

"We all make mistakes, Millicent. Beside that, it wasn't public knowledge."

"You know the press Derek, it will be soon enough. I guess

that I'll have to make some sort of public acknowledgement when that happens. I won't have a whole lot of credibility left."

"Contrition, dear Bishop. It goes far with good upstanding Christian people."

"Derek, we're talking Episcopalians here. Generally they don't care what you do, as long as they don't have to hear about it on the evening news."

"Well, you might have a point there, but hang in there. I'm sure that it will work out."

The two old friends hung up and Derek made his way back to the house. Seeing Colin and Billy on the couch in the library was like seeing Finocchio under the kitchen table—comforting that said in some way that all was right with the world. Both of them were sleeping quietly while an old movie continued in the DVD player. Derek decided to take a shower, and when he was finished, Al had come home.

"Colin and Billy still entwined on the couch?" Derek asked.

"Colin is asleep, wrapped up in a blanket, no sign of Billy."

"He must have gone upstairs to be with Daniel."

"Derek, I'm a little worried about Colin, this whole police thing has him really upset. I mean, he's not talking about it, but he just looks stressed."

"That's just it, when he's really worried about something, he *doesn't* talk about it. It's only a couple of days until the hearing and hopefully this will resolve immediately after that."

"Can you believe that guy? I can't imagine Colin even having the patience to play around with him."

"Well Al, as you should know, the mentally ill have some pretty persuasive techniques for hiding that. I don't even know when this all happened."

"It happened, dear number one spouse, during the time that you were really quite difficult to be around."

"Was I that bad?" Derek asked.

"Ask anyone in the house about that. And yes, that was another time that Colin *didn't* talk about what was bothering him."

"It didn't stop him from having a little fling with a younger Italian man, did it?"

"I said that it bothered him. You know what we all do—we

turn to our security blankets when we are under stress, and, for Colin, attractive men in their twenties are his security blanket."

"Nice way of putting it, I guess. What's on you agenda next week? I think we should have a celebratory dungeon party, what do you think?"

"When? Like Monday after the hearing?" Al asked.

"Yeah—we'll come home have dinner, a few drinks and invite the tops downstairs again. It will be fun."

"You sure that this will all work out?"

"Yeah Al, I'm sure that it will all work out. Especially now that Dominic is involved. He's not going to let anything happen to Colin."

"What are you two talking about?" Colin asked as he walked into the room, hair all askew and yawning.

"Deep theological issues," Derek teased.

"Is it still snowing?" Colin asked.

"Yes, I think that it's going to continue to pile up all through the end of February," Al answered.

The weekend passed and no one knew exactly what they did, what they said, or for that matter, what happened, except they read a lot of books, ate a lot of food that was bad for them, and basically walked on egg shells, not mentioning what was going to happen at nine o'clock on Monday morning. When Monday morning finally got there, Colin was visibly distressed, and pacing back and forth, waiting for his lawyer. Lee and Michael had joined Derek, Al, and Billy in the kitchen. They were all prepared to be witnesses. Eventually Dominic showed up and Daniel came down stairs to join the group. Finally, an hour before they had to be there, the lawyer arrived, prepped them for their parts and everyone piled into cars. It very much looked like an Italian event with the entire family showing up for what was happening to one of their own.

In the courtroom, Chris was sitting there, talking wildly to the assistant district attorney who, by that time, realized that these charges were probably not as valid as they had appeared on paper. When Colin and his entourage entered the room, Chris became more animated in his conversations with the city official. After what appeared to be hours, but was really only a few minutes, the judge appeared and Colin's case was the first to be called. All of the parties approached the judge's bench.

The police gave their report and the judge asked Chris for his side of the story. As he spoke, and accused Colin of everything that was wrong with the world, the judge looked a little skeptical, especially in the direction of the assistant district attorney, primarily to show her dislike for having to hear what she now considered a nuisance case. When asked if the police followed through on the allegations of people being held against their will in Colin's basement, they offered the pictures of the rather elaborate, and thanks to Derek, clean dungeon.

One by one, Derek, Al, Billy, Lee, and Michael offered their statements that indicating that the allegations made by Chris as to an assault were false. She finally turned her attention to Colin.

"Mr. Morgan, can you please explain this rather unusual room that you have in your basement?"

"Your honor, it is, in fact, a dungeon. I'm gay; involved in leather, and this is where we often have sexual encounters—all completely consensual. It sets the scene and acts as a prop in what can probably be thought of as role-play.

The judge was silent, and looked through the pictures. She turned to Chris and said, "Mr. Lancelotti, have you ever been held in this dungeon against your will?"

"No, your honor, but..."

"Have you even been in this dungeon, Mr. Lancelotti?"

"No, but..."

"Mr. Morgan, who do you have these role play scenarios with in this dungeon?"

Before he could answer, Derek, Al, Billy, Daniel, Lee, and Michael all said, in unison, "With me."

Eyebrows raised, and with what could only be discerned as a slight smile, the judge looked down again. When she looked up at Colin, she seemed to be choosing her words carefully. "Mr. Morgan, I'm dropping these assault charges, and I'm also not proceeding with the allegations that you have held people against their will in this... this, room of special purpose. You have the apologies of this court and this municipality for having to answer to charges that clearly have no foundation in fact. However, and I scarcely know where to begin here, by engaging in this activity, however consensual you may think that it is, you open yourself up to a whole host of potential problems. I will not comment on your lifestyle and your chosen way of engaging in sexual activity, but I will warn you that, if one person would have an issue and bring forth allegations of false imprisonment, my hands would be tied, and I would then have to proceed, and I doubt that there would be any legal way out of that. Keep that in mind before you take someone into that room. The charges are dismissed and you are released with the apologies of this court."

As they walked out of the room, Colin could feel the tension melting away. His shoulders dropped and he realized for the first time that, since that fateful night, he had been so tense that he actually changed his posture. He remained silent until they left the building, and then he let out a yell that could only be described as something between ecstasy and triumph. It caused many people on the street to turn around and look.

"Colin, be careful, we don't want a disturbing the peace citation," the attorney warned.

They went to their cars and Colin invited his attorney to join them at an early lunch. The attorney declined and said that Colin would probably change his mind about his gratitude when he saw the bill. At this point, nothing could upset Colin, he was happy to be rid of this issue.

At lunch, Colin had a few too many celebratory drinks, so much so that Dominic said that he would drive them home. As soon as they got there, Colin went upstairs and literally seemed to pass out on his bed. Apparently the huge amount of sleep that he had been getting since being arrested weren't really restful. Derek and Al were happy though; they could plan for later that night.

Lee and Michael had already declined the invitation for a dungeon party that night—Lee was still having issues with having sex with Colin in front of everyone. When Derek broached the subject with Dominic, he was appreciative, but said that he was having a date that night with one of the cops that he met in Georgia.

"You work faster than Colin," Derek said, raising an eyebrow.

"Well, we are related. But I'll disagree with you there. Colin is faster in this regard...but I'm better," Dominic said, teasing.

Derek went back into the kitchen where Billy was talking with Daniel and Al. "Are you guys up for a little dungeon-play tonight?" Derek asked.

"Fuck yeah!" Daniel answered.

"That was a little too emphatic," Billy added.

"Look guys, I was just in the woods with some very hot men. And some very not-so-hot men, and I can tell you, all I wanted was to be back here with all of you. It seemed so senseless there. It was uncomfortable and contrived and there were all of these arbitrary rules, and it was just stupid."

"Daniel, our life is often about arbitrary rules. I mean, at any given moment, Colin can switch to protocol mode and we have to follow. Most of that is arbitrary—I'm sure that you do it with Billy as well," Derek said.

"I can't explain it—yeah, you're right, all leather tops do that from time to time. But mostly, when we do it, it's for fun, or at least to assert our position. And that assertion can be feeble at times, but necessary to maintain the dynamic in our relationships. But there, it was like this group of old men got together and decided how they would promote themselves. I wish I knew more about the rest of the group, maybe they aren't *all* bad."

"What is happening with that?" Al asked.

"Well, I have to testify and so does Dominic. As of right now, only Joseph and Dave were arrested. The names of the rest of the men, including our little born-again-brother-preacher-man, were taken and will be investigated by the FBI. After that, I don't know. The police in Georgia said that there were some laws that were broken that night, but they didn't want to prosecute because of the publicity that it would bring—good or bad to the situation."

"Does anyone know about the European connection?" Derek asked.

"Dominic knows a little, and he's promised to find out more and tell us all very soon. And now he seems to be dating the really hot agent, Paul. So, I'm sure that he will get all of the information that he needs."

"Does Paul know that Dominic is connected?" Al asked.

"I'm not sure about that one, but I can honestly tell you, I'm not going to be the one to bring it up," Daniel concluded.

"Now about tonight..." Derek started and gave every man his part in the whole thing. Granted, he was being a pushy bottom in this case, but he felt that someone needed to plan the events to take place later that night. No one was cooking, dinner would be brought it, and Colin would be asked to shower, and while he's there, the boys would go downstairs and Daniel would get Colin to agree to officially reopen the dungeon.

Amazingly enough, after dinner, Colin went upstairs to take a shower. Once he was gone, Derek, Al, and Billy went downstairs, put on their leather and prepared the dungeon. Daniel went upstairs and put his leathers on. When Colin came out of the bathroom, Daniel was standing in his bedroom, in full leather.

"Feeling like you wanted to assert your position in the leather community, Daniel?" Colin asked.

"Colin, the boys would like you to get into leather and..."

"They want a dungeon party, right?" Colin finished the sentence.

"Yes, Sir, they do," Daniel answered.

"Well then, let's not keep them any longer. But, once it's over, I want to drink again."

Laughing, Daniel asked, "Is there a problem?"

"No, I just want to be numb enough to forget the past few days. Speaking of which, are you OK?"

"Yeah, I'm fine now..."

The boys were in the dungeon. They could hear the amplified steps of their Masters coming down the staircase in boots. It was dark in the basement. All of the lights were off. The faint glow of candles was coming from the back room. Strange, soft unstructured music was playing in the background. There seemed to be the smell of charcoal coming from somewhere. Colin and Daniel entered the room. The three boys fell to their knees in the center of the room.

Off to the side, Colin noticed a brazier, filled with red-hot coals and a branding iron, an old one. It was one that contained his initials, an M surrounded by a C. He smiled for a moment. Daniel already knew that it was there. Colin walked over to Derek and said, get up boy. Derek did as he was told. Colin kissed him passionately on the mouth and then went to the pegboard and pulled off a pair of nipple clamps, the kind that pinched tighter as more resistance was added to the chain connecting them. He licked Derek's nipples and then put the first one on and, after that the second. From the chain he attached a weight. Derek stood there, hands behind his back, his feet separated by the customary two feet, toes pointing forward, a good position for a slave. Colin walked back to the pegboard and pull off the parachute ball stretchers. He came back to Derek, grabbed his balls, pulled them down and attached the parachute. From this he attached an eight-pound weight. He put a blindfold on the boy and led him to the side, grabbing his arms; he attached the boy to the ceiling beam by the wrists. To his ankles, he attached new restraints and put a stretcher bar between his ankles. Derek was hanging there, at the mercy of his Master. Colin went back to Al, and told him to get up. The boy did as he was told. Colin took Al over to the sawhorse bench and attached his ankles to the one side, put a hood on the boy, bent him over, and attached his wrists to the other side. Al's ass was in the air. Colin went back to the bench and lubed up a rather strange looking butt plug. When he returned to Al, he shoved it in hard. Al let out a moan. Colin looked directly at Daniel.

Daniel took his lead and went over to Billy, "Get up," he said. Billy did as he was told. Daniel put a hood over Billy, clamped and weighted his nipples, and added weights to a ball stretcher. He led the boy over to the St. Andrew's cross and secured his wrists and his ankles to the wood. All of the boys were sufficiently restrained. Daniel returned to the center of the room, and looked longingly into Colin's eyes.

"I've loved you since the first minute I laid eyes on you, Sir," Daniel said.

"And I've grown to love you, as well," Colin answered.

The two Masters embraced each other and began deep kissing each other on the lips. Colin's hands felt the growing bulge in Daniel's crotch and soon had the other man's cock in his hand. The boys who were blindfolded or hooded in various corners of the room could feel the passion between the two men. Daniel knelt down in front of Colin and pulled out his cock. He sucked on it for a while and then leaned back, opening his mouth. Colin knew exactly what Daniel was requesting from him. It didn't take long for a steady stream of piss to spray from Colin's cock into Daniel's mouth and down over his leathers. Daniel looked ecstatic. Colin pulled him up and kissed him passionately on the mouth, tasting his own piss. He looked deeply into Daniel's eyes and then knelt in front of Daniel, taking his cock in his mouth. After a few minutes, he leaned back and assumed the position that Daniel had a few minutes earlier. Neither one of them would have done this had any of the boys been able to see what was going on. However, the boys knew that something hot was happening in the room and it gave them raging hard-ons.

Daniel sprayed his piss all over Colin, who took some in his mouth, and let some drip all over him and douse his hair as well.

Colin got up and let Daniel taste his own piss from Colin's mouth. The two men made out for a while. Colin went over to the pegboard and picked out a flogger. He returned to Derek, hanging from the ceiling beam and started gently flogging the boy. After a while, the slaps were more intense, and Derek was writhing midair. Colin went and got a butt plug and shoved it in Derek's hole. He resumed flogging the boy and making each stroke a little harder than the last. Derek was crying for mercy, but Colin would show none tonight.

Daniel did the same to Billy – except he didn't use the butt plug. Billy could take a harder flogging than Derek, but the sound of the whip make the other two boys increasingly hotter, with raging and dripping hard-ons. When Colin tired of flogging, he went over to Al and removed the butt plug. In its place it put a long, black inflatable dildo that he pumped up, and then deflated several times. Each time that he inflated the dildo, Al let out a sigh.

After a while, the boys were taken down from their restraints and were either fucked, or instructed to suck cock or eat ass, depending on what was happening at the moment. All of the men, Masters included, were horny as hell and begging for release. After about an hour, it became apparent to both Colin and Daniel that they needed some resolution. Billy knelt in between Derek and Al who faced each other. Daniel took his place behind Derek and Colin behind Al and both men fuck them hard while Billy alternated between sucking one man and then the other. He was covered in their cum after a short time, and Colin and Derek let out the groan that indicated that they had done the same into the condoms in the boys' asses.

After disengaging, Colin was standing in the middle of the room. Derek came over, knelt in front of him, and said, "Sir, this slave requests your brand." Then Al came over and said, "Sir, this slave requests your brand." Colin stared at the two men. Then the unexpected happened. Billy came over and knelt down, saying, "Sir, this slave requests your brand." Colin looked at Daniel, who didn't seem to be affected by the latest development. He merely came over to Colin, kissed him on the mouth and said, "Sir, the Master requests your brand as well." Colin was speechless, but knew that he had to act quickly, or the moment would pass.

He took Derek over to the bench and bent him over. He retrieved some disinfectant from the table, washed off an area of Derek's butt, and got the branding iron. He touched the skin for a second, which caused Derek to cry out. Then he returned the iron to the coals. Al was next, and Colin repeated the process. When Billy was over the bench, Colin got the iron and handed it to Daniel who did the honors. Then, Daniel pulled down his leather jeans and bent over the bench. The three boys turned to face the wall—they wouldn't watch a Master submit, even to another Master. Colin grabbed the iron, went over in front of Daniel, lifted his head, and kissed him passionately on the lips. He then returned to the other side of the bench and touched the red-hot branding iron to the skin of Daniel's butt. The man let out a yell.

The five of them were silent for several minutes. Finally, Colin decided to break the spell, "Boys, you need to clean up this area and yourselves. And you need to put some ointment on those burns. Daniel and I are going upstairs to do the same. We'll see you in a couple of hours." Daniel and Colin left the room, removed their leathers for the boys to clean, and went upstairs.

Once upstairs, they jumped in the shower together. In many ways, the scene in the shower was just as hot as what happened in the dungeon downstairs. Colin and Daniel were all over each other. The two of them kissed deeply as the water coursed over their bodies, and both men were erect again.

"Why did you do that, let me band you?" Colin asked.

"Well, it just seemed right. Today, when Derek and Al were discussing it, Billy looked a little forlorn. When we got a chance to be together, I knew what he wanted. He wouldn't tell, me, but I just knew. I asked him if he wanted to be branded by you, and he said yes."

"But you…you're a Master, I respect that," Colin said.

"I know, but Colin, I love you so much. It's incredible. I'm not sure where this is leading, and I don't know if Billy and I are in this family as full members or associates, but I wanted it."

"I've never had a more intensely sexual moment in my life," Colin said. "Don't let me forget to put something on that brand before we go to bed tonight."

Downstairs, the boys were cleaning up, each of them wincing a little from the burn on their butt cheeks. There was a lot to clean up, but they were talking among themselves as they did it.

"So, I heard pissing, who do you think pissed on whom?" Al asked.

"I bet Colin pissed all over Daniel as some sort of initiation," Billy added.

"I don't know, I couldn't tell, I just know that it happened a couple of times," Derek said.

"Do you think that we will ever know?" Al asked.

"Probably not, but what do you think about Daniel being branded?" Derek asked.

"Does that mean that we're part of the family now?" Billy asked.

"You always have been," Derek said, and continued cleaning. Outside the door, they found the wet leathers and took them, cleaned them, and conditioned them and then took a communal shower. After that, Al put antiseptic cream all over the burn marks on their butts, and then Derek did his. "These look so cool," Derek said.

After a few more minutes, the boys joined the Masters upstairs, in Colin's bedroom. Like always, Colin and Daniel were making out. They all joined the two on the bed. Everyone was in a good mood, they were all relaxed and didn't seem to have a care in the world. Each one of them was trying to assess the significance of the scene downstairs and what it meant; were Daniel and Billy equal partners in this relationship? Were Derek and Al to answer to Daniel? Between Colin and Daniel, which one was answerable to which one? No one knew, and, while it was something that they all pondered, they each realized that it was nothing to loose sleep over.

It was sleep that ended the night. All five of them somehow managed to arrange themselves comfortably on the bed and that's where they fell asleep. It was the deep sleep of men who had resolved all of their issues and were fulfilled in every way. They didn't know what lay ahead for them, or the direction that the family was taking, but they were so content being in the presence of each other.

Chapter 21

The next morning, no one was going to work from the leather household. They were all completely exhausted. Colin had been calling in for the past week, Al had been 'doing research at home', Billy *rarely* needed to be at work, and Daniel was still on leave. He had taken some extended time, not knowing how long the issue with the leather club would take, but architecture firms were often quite forgiving of personal issues. Derek woke early the next morning, as was his custom and decided to go over to the church offices to take care of loose ends. There would be a lot, he was kind of ignoring the parish for the past couple of weeks, and genuinely felt bad about that. However, he wasn't prepared for what waited for him. Millicent was literally sitting on the stoop to the back door of the parish offices.

"Well, this is unusual, I don't usually find Bishops waiting on the steps," Derek said.

"Oh Derek, this is a real mess, can we talk?"

They went inside, and Derek made coffee with the machine in his outer office. He brought two steeping mugs into the room and sat down at his desk, Millicent opposite him.

"What has happened?" Derek asked.

"Well, the standing committee had a special meeting to discuss the 'situation' of the bishop and the televangelist caught diddling in the woods in Georgia."

"They can't blame you for his weaknesses, can they?" Derek asked.

"No, but they can blame me for my lack of judgment."

"You didn't marry him, for crying out loud. I don't think that you're giving your counselors the credit that they deserve."

"Oh Derek, I just feel so...so...so defeated. How could I

have been blinded by the man?"

"Not just you Millicent, think of all of his followers. His adamant condemnation of homosexuality, and his proclivities for a subculture within that larger group…a subculture that sometimes even mainstream homosexuals don't understand."

"What will I do, how can I withstand the scandal that is bound to come out. Someone must have seen us having dinner and looking very much, the couple in love."

"I have some experience with scandal, and I can tell you this. It passes and so does the sting of the scandal. You'll be surprised in a year how all of this seemed as significant as it does now."

The two old friends said goodbye and Derek went back to answer phone calls, emails, and generally deal with any issues that arose while he was preoccupied with his life. Episcopal parishes could run themselves for a time, but the rector was always the anchor—the rock upon which the local church built its foundation. He would have to decide soon whether he wanted to devote more time to the parish, and less to his position in a leather family or vice versa. He knew which one he would pick if he had his choice.

When Derek got back to the house, everyone was up. Billy had been sent to the local bakery for sweet roles and the coffee brewing here smelled much richer than the pot he had brewed over in the church offices. It was good to see his entire family gathered, once again, around the kitchen table. It gave him a sense of calm and continuity.

"Where were you?" Colin asked.

"Over at the church seeing what was happening while I've been trying to deal with all of our issues here," Derek answered.

"Was there much that needed your attention?" Al asked.

"Well, my bishop was waiting for my attention, literally camped out on the porch."

"How is Millicent?" Colin asked.

"Millicent is in turmoil, and she'll just have to work through it herself," Derek answered as a knock came to the back door. It was open, so Dominic strolled on in, seeing everyone in his favorite spot.

"Hey guys, what's up?" Dominic asked.

"How was your date?" Colin asked in return.

"It was great, I can't believe it; he's such a nice guy."

"Where is he?" Al asked.

"He had to go back to Pittsburgh—this was just a whimsical thing last night. And it made me very happy," Dominic answered.

"Does he know about your rather other life, the private life?" Colin asked.

"Yeah, he knows. It's a problem, but not one that is irresolvable."

"I don't want to know," was all that Colin said.

"So, how is everyone over here?" Dominic asked.

"We are just super," Billy said, coming in the back door laden with sweets from the local bakery.

The rest of the morning was spent eating, drinking, and telling the stories of the latest great adventures. And then, of course, there were the retellings of the stories from different perspectives. As they were sitting around, beginning to think about lunch, there was a knock at the front door. Billy went to answer it and came back within a minute or two with a very distinguished man dressed a little strangely—at least a little strangely for America, he looked very much like a proper Bavarian gentlemen somewhere between forty and fifty years old. All eyes turn to him.

"I'm very sorry to bother you all," he said with a thick Bavarian accent. "But I wanted to come by and tell all of you how sorry we, the executive board of the Dark Knights of St. Germaine, are about the recent unpleasantness here in your country. And I know that it affected you all personally. We had no knowledge of these men or their particular problems. We would certainly have never let them join our ranks. I apologize especially to you Colin, and to you, Dominic," the man said looking at both men. This caused them a little concern.

"How do you know that I'm Colin, and that my cousin is the man over there?" Colin asked, standing up.

"Oh, sorry. You don't remember me. My name is Wolfgang, I was present when Heinrich initiated you into our way of life and gave you leather to wear. I look much differently now."

"I think that I might remember you," Colin said. "But it has been a long time, we've all changed."

"You haven't changed much yet...but, don't worry, that will

happen in a few years. You will loose that youthful look, like we all do."

Colin wasn't sure if he should be offended, or simply amused at the stark German sensibility of this man. As he looked more closely at Wolfgang, he thought that he could remember that night in Bavaria when he was subjected to all sorts of humiliation before being given his leathers. Finally he said to Wolfgang, "How long are you here in Columbus? Would you like to stay with us and remember old times?"

"I'm afraid that I won't be able to do that. I have to give a statement to your authorities on the nature of our club, and, I'm seeing Heinrich's old boy and giving him the rest of the German estate left to him. Have you seen him lately?"

"Well, not for about a year or so, but somehow even without communicating we've remained close."

"You know that he was willed to you, Colin."

The eyes that were darting back and forth around the table could cause a person to become disoriented. Derek, Al, Billy and Daniel were each giving each other sidelong glances. The only one that didn't seem affected by the last statement, besides Colin, was Dominic.

"Yes, I know, Wolfgang, but now is not the time or place for that. It may come to that soon, but now, we wait. I assume that you will be helping him find his way?"

"I understand *mein Herr*, and yes, I will be talking to him about that," the composed German said. "But now, I must be going."

Colin got up and gave Wolfgang a hug, and then Dominic followed suit. After very cordial goodbyes were said, Colin and Dominic walked the gentleman to the front, and went with him to his rented car, a Mercedes. He drove off and the two men returned to the warmth of the kitchen.

"It's real! All of those stories you've told about Heinrich is real," Derek said.

"Of course, little one. Why would you think that they weren't real? For what would I make up a story like that."

"Who is this Mario guy that you've inherited?" Al asked, clearly a little concerned that another Italian was possibly in the mix.

"A very hot man, who is one of the most proficient bottoms I've ever met," Dominic said, answering the question for his cousin.

"Well, if he's hot enough, you can just bring him onboard," Billy said as he sat down. He winced when his butt hit the chair; he had managed to sit right down on the spot where Colin had branded him.

"What's wrong with you, a little too much paddling last night?" Dominic asked.

"You don't know? I was branded," Billy added, "We all were."

"Daniel branded you? Dominic asked.

"No, Colin branded us."

Dominic looked a little confused. Finally, he said, "So Colin branded you and Derek and Al all on the same night? With Daniel's permission?"

"He branded me as well," Daniel said.

Dominic clearly looked a little confused. "Well, I guess that it was good that I was busy. I don't think I'm ready to be branded by you," he said, looking at Colin.

"What does it mean? Are you a really big leather family now?" Dominic continued.

"I can't speak for everyone, but we're connected to each other. I don't know if that means that we are all together on the same level, or that there are two distinct levels here with a lot of interaction between them. I just don't know," Colin said, looking at all of the men for some kind of affirmation.

"It's comfortable, having us all here and breaking down the barriers that separate us. I'm sure that we are going to have to come up with some rules, and we have two Masters here, so that won't be a problem. I guess that decisions will be a little more complicated and that matters will take a little longer to resolve," Al added.

"I guess that we're rewriting the rules here. I'm excited. And I assume that we will continue, for the most part, status quo, Billy sleeping with Daniel and the three of us together. Of course, Billy and Colin often have little engagements, but we don't mention that," Derek said.

"I'm totally blown away by this. Yeah, the three-way relationship was a little avant-garde but a logical progression, especially in the leather world. Adding two more, in whatever capacity is almost utopia," Dominic said.

"And you know, Dominic..." Colin said.

"You don't even have to say it, I already know that I'm welcome here. But, for right now, I need a one on one and to deal with my demons. That's not to say that I don't want to remain close to you guys, or that I don't want to have sex with you all from time to time, but I need to build on a promising new relationship."

"Well, let's try to stay together—at least in the same hemisphere. And maybe someday, we can all be together," Colin said, putting his hand on Dominic's shoulder.

"Didn't the Supremes sing something about that?" Daniel joked.

"Yeah, and when is this Mario joining us?" Billy asked.

Everyone started laughing. Even Colin laughed at that one. "Mario has his own demons to deal with and his own issues to bury. Heinrich took him to the very edge of existence and brought him back. When Heinrich died, it left a void that wasn't easily filled. Mario has gone to great lengths to try to discover for himself who he is. He submits to Masters who often don't have his best interests at heart, but he is watched by many from the old days, apparently even leather men from Germany. In time, when Mario comes to peace with everything in his life, he will come, and I will claim my inheritance."

"I hate to break the magic of this moment, but what about the job in Pittsburgh?" Derek asked.

"Don't worry, I phoned Mary Rose this morning and put it on hold—permanently. I didn't decline, but simply said that this was a bad time for something like that. I think we have enough to figure out here. And you Derek, what are you going to do? Be a priest? Think of something else to do?"

"I'm not sure. I'm content, for once; we'll have to see. I guess that we will go with the flow for a little while."

"Yeah, I'm going to go with the flow as well," Billy said. All of the men laughed. "I just can't believe that I live in a house with a bunch of men I have sex with and a little Italian hottie next door who has a hot cop boyfriend, one that I haven't seen yet, and I get to do this every day. Who could have thought of anything better than that?"

"Now that the evil leather men are behind us, we can certainly breathe a sigh of relief and get on with our lives again," Daniel added.

"When is the trial?" Al asked.

"I don't know. I guess that we'll find out," Dominic answered. "And I guess that we will find out what happened to the Reverend Mark Marjoram and the consequences that it will have for Millicent. For once, life in gay-dom seems to be resolved and life in the straight world is all a twitter with uncertainty."

"Yeah—we won this one. But, the way that politics are evolving in this country, we never know, we may have to move to have simple rights someday," Colin said.

"I've been thinking about that a lot. I have some property in Canada, we could develop it, make a big huge house as a get-away and, at the very least, go there when we *need* to get away," Dominic added. "Besides, with the number of lovers that you have, dear cousin, it wouldn't take much capital from each person to build a castle there—just north of Toronto."

"This is totally great. I have a bunch of hot men around me, and maybe someday I'll have a castle," Billy said. I guess that old guy was right, all's well that end's well."

"Billy, it isn't ending, it's only beginning," Colin said.

The Beginning

About the Author

Chuck Williams was born in Pennsylvania in the 1950s. He attended university and several graduate schools, never quite deciding on what he wanted to do with his life. Introduced to leather in the late seventies, he became one of those men dressed completely in black leather, hidden by the shadows in leather bars across the world. While reading and writing are two of his passions, he actually makes his living in the scientific community. He currently lives in Pittsburgh with his lover, Michael, and a very, very bad dog.

www.ingramcontent.com/pod-product-compliance
Lightning Source LLC
Chambersburg PA
CBHW071219260626
47162CB00004B/1362

* 9 7 8 1 8 8 7 8 9 5 1 9 4 *